Ignite Her Fire
(Love After I Do)
by
Zena Wynn
©2024

A Real Love Enterprises Publication

ISBN 978-1-958215-19-7

ZENA WYNN

IGNITE HER FIRE

Twenty years of marriage. One overheard confession that shatters everything. Grant and Sasha's marriage is tested when Grant overhears Sasha's admission: I've never had an orgasm. Grant's world crumbles. After this ego destroying revelation, can they find their way back to the passionate love he thought they once shared? Or will Grant lose the only woman he's ever loved to someone who knows how to Ignite Her Fire?

Chapter One

Grant

"I've never had an orgasm."

I froze mid-step, certain I'd heard wrong. I'd no sooner backed the car out of the garage to drive to Home Depot when I realized I'd left my credit card sitting on my computer keyboard. Hopping out of the car, I ducked under the closing garage door to dash into the house to grab it. I was headed out again when I overheard Sasha's comment.

"I mean I enjoy sex, but I've never had anything close to the orgasms described in the erotic romance you gave me to read," Sasha said.

I breathed a sigh of relief. If my wife was comparing our sex life to some silly romance novel, no wonder it hadn't measured up. Dismissing her conversation, I continued forward to the door. Her next words made me pause with my hand on the doorknob.

"Sex is..." Sasha made the humming noise she unconsciously made whenever she carefully chose her words. "It's nice, pleasant...comfortable, like sinking into a hot bath at the end of a long tiring day. It feels good but..."

Nice? Pleasant? *Comfortable?* "What the hell?"

I must have spoken aloud because Sasha suddenly said, "Hold on, Peggy. I heard something."

I immediately flattened against the wall and held my breath. *Don't come this way! Don't come this way!* I mentally chanted.

In the silence, I imagined Sasha tilting her head to the side and listening. After a few nerve-racking seconds, she said, "I'm back. I thought I heard a man's voice. It sounded really close. ... No, it wasn't Grant. He isn't home. ... What? ... No, Peggy, I don't think someone broke into our house in the few minutes Grant's been gone. This is a safe neighborhood. We have several cops living on the block and scattered throughout the subdivision." The last was said absently, telling me Sasha was still focused on the source of the sound she'd heard.

The soft fall of Sasha's footsteps on the tile floor came closer to where I hid. I scurried back until I was out of sight, just inside my office door. Fuck. I wanted to hear the rest of this conversation. Suddenly, our next-door neighbor's souped-up car engine revved and loud Spanish music blared, echoing throughout the house. It was the one thing I hated most about our subdivision. The damned houses were built right on top of each other. For the first time, I was grateful.

Sasha gave a soft chuckle. "Mystery solved. I must have heard Rodrigo, our next-door neighbor. That's so weird. It sounded like he was right in the house with me. Listen, I'm going to put you on speakerphone so I can wash dishes," Sasha said.

I eased out of the office and crept down the short hallway, past the half-bath, and closer to the kitchen. Staying hidden with my back to the wall, I peeked around the corner. The short hallway exited into a large, airy foyer and formal dining room, beyond which was the kitchen. The foyer's cathedral ceiling and lack of doors provided excellent acoustics and let even murmured conversations be heard clearly in other parts of the house.

"Where's Grant?" Peggy's voice came over the speaker, heard clearly above the water running into the kitchen sink.

"He went to the hardware store."

"So, you finally read one of the books I gave you. I've only been nagging you for months," Peggy said.

"I know. I was busy trying to get Wendi off to college. Then Nigel came home on leave. Things were hectic and didn't leave time for relaxing with a good book." Sasha's footsteps paced back and forth as she cleared the breakfast dishes from the table.

I wanted to move closer but if I stepped out into the open, she'd see me.

"Honey, there's always time to read, even if it's on the john. Which one did you read, and how did you like it?" Peggy asked, her voice showing her enthusiasm.

"Can't remember the title, but it was the book about a man who could turn into a bear. I think they called them shifters? Anyway, it surprised me how much I enjoyed it. I couldn't believe the way her family treated the heroine. I take back what I said about erotic romances being nothing but soft porn."

Would you forget about the damned book and get back to talking about sex? I silently demanded.

"I told you there was more to romance novels than sex. See what you've been missing by limiting your reading to cozy mysteries and true crime?" The clinking of dishes being rinsed filled the void as the conversation paused. "You've *never* had an orgasm?" Peggy's voice held a note of incredulity. "Does Grant know?"

Thank you, Peggy, for bringing the conversation back to what I wanted to hear.

"Grant and I don't discuss our sex life," Sasha said, her tone matter-of-fact.

"I thought you two talked about everything. Why not this?"

I peeked around the corner again. No sign of Sasha. It sounded like she was loading the dishwasher, which meant her back would be to me. My feet silent on the tiled floor, I skirted around the corner and darted to the wall on the right side of the arch leading into the kitchen/living room combo. With my back to the wall, I could neither see nor be seen unless Sasha decided to go upstairs. Then I was screwed.

"I don't know. Sex is something we've always just done. Who talks about their sex life?" Sasha asked, her raised voice a sign of her growing agitation.

"Plenty do, but I see what you're saying. Once a couple becomes lovers, the conversations about sex reduce to when to do it, finding time to do it, or if one of them is adventurous, convincing the other to try something new. But, Sasha, if you're not being satisfied, you should discuss it with Grant," Peggy said.

"I never said I wasn't satisfied. After all, we've been married for over twenty years. Even so, I can't just walk up to Grant and say, '*By the way, honey, I read this book and now I'm starting to wonder if I've ever had an orgasm.*' It would hurt him, not to mention the damage it would do to his ego. He'd think it was his fault."

"Are you sure it's not?" Peggy asked.

The muscles in my neck and shoulders tensed as I awaited her answer. God, how I wanted to storm into the kitchen and demand answers. The need to act had my adrenaline racing.

There was a loud thump as Sasha forcibly loaded one of the dishes into the dishwasher. Her voice was firm when she said, "Grant's a wonderful, considerate lover. If there's a problem, I'm sure it's me. I did a little research on the subject. Not all women are capable of climaxing. Maybe I'm one of them."

"Hogwash! Every woman can orgasm. Our bodies are built for pleasure. Some women simply don't know how. Or because of stress, they can't relax long enough to let it happen naturally, but mostly it's because men are selfish jerks who don't care about anyone's satisfaction but their own," Peggy said.

"Grant's not like that. I told you, he's a wonderful, considerate lover."

Sasha's vehemence eased something tight in my chest. I didn't think I was a selfish lover, but having my wife confirm it helped.

"All right, all right. Just checking. No need to get hostile. I was just saying. Still, how would you know? You said Grant was your first lover, and that you'd been together since high school. It's not like you have a comparison."

Sasha turned off the faucet and silence filled the room. Finally, in a measured tone that showed her patience was being stretched, she said, "Peggy, I never said Grant was my only lover."

I jerked and took a step forward before catching myself. *What the hell?*

"You had an affair?" Peggy's voice echoed the shocked disbelief I felt. There was no way my wife had cheated on me. Sasha was too honorable.

"No! I did not cheat on my husband!" Sasha said forcefully.

"If you didn't have an affair, what happened?" Peggy said.

"It's a long story," Sasha said, obviously reluctant to go into it.

I made a "get on with it" motion with my hand. Don't get quiet now, babe. Inquiring minds need to know.

"I've got nothing but time." When Sasha didn't immediately respond, Peggy cajoled, "Come on, Sasha. You can't leave me hanging. Best friends, remember?"

I imagined Sasha standing at the kitchen island, staring at her phone while the dishwasher hummed gently in the background. She'd chew her lower lip as she debated how much to say. I stared through the wall, mentally willing her to share what Peggy and I both wanted to know.

With a long sigh, Sasha capitulated. "Grant proposed while we were still in high school."

"But I thought you two didn't get married until after college graduation?" Peggy said.

"That's because when we made our big announcement, our parents did not approve. His mother suggested we wait a few years and date other people. His dad spouted statistics about how many teenage marriages end in divorce. My dad said he'd pay for the wedding if we waited until after we'd both graduated from college. Bottom line, everyone thought we were too young," Sasha said.

"I wish someone would have objected when I was hellbent on marrying Tom," Peggy said.

Would you quit interrupting her? I wanted to shout. *No one cares about you and Tom.*

"Now that I'm older, I can better understand their position and would most likely say the same to Wendi or Nigel. Anyway, I argued, but Grant caved under the pressure. We separated for a few years and got back together the summer before our senior year. During that time, I had a few short relationships. Nothing that ever became serious," Sasha said.

"Oh my god, I never knew that. Does Grant know?"

I closed my eyes as her words sank in. The idea that Sasha might have had other lovers never crossed my mind. I'd been too full of myself back then. Too certain of her love for me to think she'd do more than casually date to satisfy our parents' wishes. Even though it had been decades since she'd been with another man, it didn't stop the jealous rage coursing through me.

"I don't know." I could hear the unconcern in Sasha's voice. "One of the rules Grant insisted on when we got back together was that we not discuss anything we did with others during our break. Besides, it wasn't like he had room to judge. We attended the same university. Despite our traveling in different social circles, every time I saw Grant he was with a different girl. For a while, he was the talk of the campus. That's really what pushed me into accepting dates with other guys."

The reminder of all the girls I'd gone through put a chokehold on my unreasonable jealousy.

"I take none of the others rang your bell?" Peggy asked.

Sasha chuckled softly. "They were nice guys, barely more experienced than me, but eager to please. Sex was okay, but my feelings for Grant kept getting in the way. I usually broke things off after a few months before the guys could get too attached. Being with me when I was hung up on Grant wasn't fair to them."

"Soooo, what are you going to do?" Peggy asked.

"About what?"

"About what?" Peggy sputtered. "About this whole never having an orgasm thing."

"Nothing."

"Nothing?"

Sasha sighed. "What do you want me to do, Peggy?"

Peggy sputtered some more before admitting, "I don't know, but aren't you curious about what you're missing?"

Sasha's voice moved closer. I edged closer to the closet, wondering if I'd have to dive inside of it to keep from being spotted.

"Well, yes, but marriage is about more than sex. Grant and I have a great relationship and a wonderful marriage. He's more than my husband; he's my best friend. I'm not going to screw that up over a bit of curiosity," Sasha said.

Peggy sighed. "You've got a point. You know, there are things you can do to educate yourself."

Brows lowered in suspicion, I wondered, things like what? Of all women, I didn't want Sasha getting sex advice from Peggy. The woman had become unhinged since her divorce.

"Like what?" Sasha asked, her tone cautious.

"Sex toys, for one. There are plenty designed by women to maximize a woman's pleasure. I can recommend a few," Peggy offered.

"I don't think–" Sasha began.

"Or, I can help you like Denise helped me. She taught me how to learn my body. Explore my sexuality. I'd love to teach you how to pleasure yourself. You're a very passionate woman. All you need is the right person to light your fire," Peggy said, her tone husky.

Wait a damn minute. Was Peggy coming on to my wife?

"Uh..." Sasha said, clearly uncomfortable with the direction the conversation had taken.

"Think about it. Gotta go. Denise is calling me. We're spending the day at the spa." Peggy sighed. "She's so romantic. Unlike that pig I divorced. Before I run off, what's next on your reading list?"

Sasha laughed. I don't know if Peggy heard her relief at the change of subject, but I did. "A contemporary suspense I already have loaded onto my tablet. As soon as I finish cleaning, I plan to kick back and read."

I took a chance and peeked past the arch. I couldn't see Sasha from this angle. Unable to wait a moment longer, I rushed to the front door, expecting to be spotted any moment. I eased the door open and closed it silently behind me. As I drove off, Sasha's conversation twirled around in my thoughts. What, if anything, was I going to do about her revelation?

Chapter Two

Sasha

With a sigh of relief, I closed my phone and set it on the island. On autopilot, I finished wiping down the countertops and table before rinsing the dishrag and hanging it on the faucet to dry. Then I stood in front of the sink, staring out the kitchen window at the manmade pond.

I liked Peggy. We'd been extremely close for over sixteen years, but this last year things had been...strained. The bonds that held our friendship together had slowly unraveled until not much remained. Still, I'd held on. After today's conversation, I was finally ready to admit that it might be time to let go.

Peggy and I met at a summer picnic hosted by Grant's company. Peggy's husband, Tom, had also been a new hire with the fiduciary firm. While Grant had been with the company longer, having interned with them during college, both men were the same age. As young wives with young children in a crowd of much older families, we'd gravitated together. Over the years, we'd become fast friends, socialized as couples, and even vacationed together.

Two years ago, Peggy had caught Tom cheating with a woman almost the same age as their daughter. I'd been her crutch, supporting her through the painful implosion of her marriage and acrimonious divorce. With her divorce finalized and her children legally of age, Peggy had embarked on a year-long quest to, in her words, "find out what I missed while chained to the pig." Between online dating sites, clubbing, sex clubs, and now a lesbian lover—I didn't think there was a sexual avenue my friend hadn't explored.

Peggy's wild escapades hadn't disturbed me. We'd both married right out of college and had children early in life. Like me, Peggy had been a mostly stay-at-home mom with the occasional foray into the workforce to keep her skills sharp and resume relevant. While I found her leap into lesbianism confusing, Peggy's children were grown and gone from home, and her actions hurt no one.

Tom's betrayal had destroyed her confidence in herself as a woman. As a result, she'd latched onto her new lifestyle with the desperation and fervor of a religious convert. While sympathetic to her plight, I had to draw the line when she'd tried pushing her opinions of men onto me, and in the process, infect my marriage with her bitterness. Not every man was a liar and a cheat. She'd toned it down quite a bit after I confronted her, but the occasional toxic comment still slipped out.

Her drastically altered lifestyle combined with her toxic attitude towards men meant we no longer talked as frequently. It had been weeks since we'd last spoken. I'd reached out today to let her know I'd finally read one of the books she'd recommended and found myself blurting out a confession that had been troubling me for days. Once the words were out, no matter how much I desperately wished otherwise, there'd been no taking them back.

I wandered into the living room, straightened the pillows on the couch, and ran a finger along the mantle to check for dust. Deciding that dusting could wait another week, I pulled out the vacuum and cleaned the rug. All the while, my conversation with Peggy continued to play through my mind.

I might not be as sexually open as Peggy, but I was no prude. Still, her offer to teach me how to pleasure myself had shocked me to my core. I'd never had a woman come on to me, and as a result, my response had been less than graceful. That the woman who tried it had been Peggy, of all people, showed just how much she'd changed.

I'd been hoping our friendship would gradually get back to normal as she healed from Tom's betrayal. That was looking less and less likely. Peggy liked to party. The staid couples' dates of dinner and a movie we'd enjoyed in the past she now considered boring. We were both still mothers, but both our nests were empty and Peggy rarely mentioned her children. We were entering new phases in our lives. After her divorce, our circle of friends had changed. The only thing left was our love of reading. I'd been hoping it would be enough to bridge the growing gap, but now...?

Despite Peggy's disbelief, Grant and I had a solid marriage. I loved the intimacy and connection I experienced during sex with my husband. I might be a tad curious about what I'd been missing—okay, extremely curious since reading Peggy's book—but I'd never admit it to her. If she brought up the subject again, I'd feign ignorance. I didn't want a repeat of today's offer.

Even so, Peggy had made one interesting point. It wouldn't hurt to explore my body and learn how to pleasure myself. There'd been times while making love with Grant that I'd felt a sharp bite of...something. It was too fierce to be called pleasure. I felt like I was coming out of my skin. The sensation had been so intense, I'd wanted to scratch, claw, and scream. To beg for Grant to stop even as I demanded that he continue.

Shocked to the core at the violence of my reaction, I'd held back and been left feeling bereft, almost empty when our lovemaking ended. The descriptive sex scenes in the romances I'd read caused me to realize I might have been close to a powerful orgasm. In my ignorance, and yes, fear, I'd cheated both myself and Grant of something special. Somehow, someway, I had to learn how to get past the fear, let go, and allow myself to orgasm.

Sighing, I glanced around. My Saturday chores were completed, Grant would be home any minute, and I was tired of thinking heavy thoughts. It was a beautiful fall day outside. The sun shone with nary a cloud to hide it, and a nice breeze kept the humidity low. All in all, a perfect day for relaxing on the lanai with a good book.

Grant and I had shared a fairly substantial breakfast of pancakes, bacon, and eggs less than an hour ago. Despite not being hungry, I made myself a snack of buttery popcorn and poured a glass of lemonade. I placed everything on a tray and added a bottle of water.

With my tablet under one arm and the tray in hand, I carried everything out to the lanai and set it on one of the couch cushions in easy reach. I settled on the outdoor patio furniture and put my feet on an ottoman. This was the part of the day I enjoyed most.

According to my e-reader, I had about an hour's reading time left in my book. I'd been engrossed in the story last night before bed when Grant had given me "the look." The one that said sex was on his mind and didn't I want to come play? Since I'd much rather have sex with my husband than read about fictional characters, I'd ditched the tablet and accepted Grant's unspoken invitation.

I opened up the story to the point where I left off and got comfortable. Soon, I was so immersed in the climatic ending, I lost all awareness of my surroundings. The conclusion had me sagging into the couch and staring blankly outside as I waited for my mind to transition back to reality.

As I sipped from my bottle of water, I contemplated going into the kitchen to take meat out of the freezer to defrost for dinner. I'd meant to do it earlier, but my conversation with Peggy put it out of my mind. While debating if I really felt like moving, I absently scrolled through the other books in my library until one of the covers caught my eye. I clicked on book details to read the blurb. Hmm, it sounded interesting. I downloaded the story and opened it to the first chapter, intending to read a page or two before taking out the meat. That was the last thought I had as the opening scene sucked me in...

————

The phone rang multiple times and went to voicemail. I disconnected before the message could play and called again. Same response. I hit redial. No answer. "Damn it, Mom. You said you'd be ready. I don't have time for this."

I tossed the phone into my purse, grabbed my cane, and struggled my way out of the rental SUV. I still wasn't used to maneuvering with the cane, despite being in the leg brace for over a week. Fire streaked through my leg as I put weight on it. Pausing to breathe through the pain, I adjusted my purse strap over my shoulder before hobbling forward enough to close the car door.

I swear, my mother would be late to her own funeral. I'd texted and told her I was on the way. An accident on the interstate highway had diverted traffic, adding fifteen minutes to my travel time. She should have been standing at the window, watching for me. With gritted teeth and a stream of muttered curses, I made my way up the sidewalk.

Keeping my knee straight while climbing the twenty stairs to the second floor was a bitch. It had to be at least ninety degrees in the shade, and the bright sun shining down on me felt like a heat lamp. The lack of breeze and stifling humidity made breathing difficult. Sweat coated my face when I finally reached the top. I paused for a minute, trying to catch my breath and waited for the pain in my leg to subside.

A glance at my watch told me if we didn't leave now, we'd be late for mom's appointment. Still cursing, I limped towards the door. It never failed. No matter how early I arrived in an effort to be on time, mom always found a way to make us late.

"Sorry, Raine, I lost track of time..."

"Just let me do one more thing and then we can leave..."

"Honey, can we make a quick stop? I promise it won't take more than a minute..."

Too annoyed to dig into my bag for mom's keys, I pounded on the wood door. The door swung open on silent hinges, and a waft of cold air drifted over me. A sense of unease washed over me. It wasn't like mom to leave her door unlocked.

"Mom?" Had she started out the door, realized she'd forgotten something, and gone back inside to retrieve it?

"Mom?" I called a little louder.

No response. The feeling of wrongness scraped along my nerve endings and raised the hair on my arms. Years of watching Crime TV kept me hovering on the threshold, reluctant to enter. The condo was too silent. My mother liked noise and always kept the television or music playing in the background when she was home. It was the first thing she turned on when she walked into the condo and the last thing she turned off when leaving.

Adrenalin surged as my fight-or-flight response kicked in. Caution warred with the need to act. Following my intuition, I took out my phone and dialed nine-one-one.

"Nine-one-one, what's your emergency?"

"Hi, um, I was supposed to meet my mom to take her to her doctor's appointment. I spoke with her an hour ago, but now she's not answering her phone. When I arrived at her condo, I found the front door open. That's not like her. My mother's very safety conscious."

"Address of the emergency?"

I gave the operator the address and apartment number.

"Have you entered the dwelling?" the operator said.

"No. Look, something's wrong. I feel it in my gut. Can you just send someone, please?"

"I'm routing someone to you. You said your mother had a doctor's appointment?"

"Yes, with her cardiologist. She had a heart attack six months ago, but she's a lot better now. This is just a routine checkup." I used my cane to push the door wider, giving me a better view of the interior.

"There's an officer in the area. Don't enter the apartment. I need you to stay on the line until they arrive."

———

The sound of the garage door opening pulled me out of the story. I glanced at my watch, surprised to see how late it was. Grant had been gone for hours. My gaze drifted back to my tablet and was immediately captured. I continued reading...

———

"I'm sure I'm worrying for nothing. It's just that a lot of weird shit's been happening lately. I see her purse on the kitchen island. Maybe she's in the master bathroom at the back of the condo and can't hear me. Mom!"

I called out again, moving the phone away from my mouth so I wouldn't yell in the operator's ear.

"The patrol car should be there any moment. Don't enter the apartment," the operator repeated.

"I won't." Despite my promise, I slowly walked in, as though being drawn forward by an invisible rope. From the entryway, all I could see of the open-plan condo was the dining room and kitchen. The living room and master bedroom were just out of view to the right.

"Do you see the patrol car? He's in the complex," the operator said.

Halfway into the condo, I saw a portion of my mother's lower body sprawled on the floor. She had one shoe on and the other lay nearby on its side as though she'd fallen while putting on her shoes.

"Oh, God. Tell the officer to hurry. Mom's been hurt." I rushed forward only to stop in horror as my stunned gaze took in the blood. It was everywhere—the furniture, the walls, and there was a huge puddle under her body, staining the cream carpet red. My eyes focused on the large butcher knife handle sticking out between my mother's ribs, and I screamed...

———

"Sasha, can we talk?"

"Hmm?" I asked, eyes still glued to the tablet.

———

The nine-one-one operator yelling in my ear snapped me out of my shock. By some miracle, I hadn't dropped the phone. "Oh, God. Oh, God. The blood. It's everywhere."

Some dim part of me recognized that my mother was beyond help, but the child in me refused to believe. Nobody could lose this much blood and survive.

"Whose blood?" the operator asked.

"My mother. She's on the floor. There's a knife in her chest," I sobbed, barely able to choke the words out.

"Is she breathing?"

"I don't know. I can't tell. There's so much blood. My God, who would do this? Why is this happening to me?" I cried, unable to tear my gaze from my mother's ashen face. First, it was my roommate, Raine. Then it was my boyfriend, Tom. One by one, the people I loved were slowly being taken away from me.

———

"Sasha!"

The snap in Grant's tone had me jerking upright in my seat, story forgotten. One glance at his grim expression had me tossing the tablet aside and surging to my feet. "What's wrong? Is it the kids? Did something happen while you were out?"

"We need to talk."

Heart hammering, I watched Grant stalk onto the patio, searching for signs of what he needed to discuss. Everything had been fine earlier. We'd eaten breakfast. Grant had disappeared into his office to clear up a few things for work. I'd been cleaning the kitchen when he'd stuck his head in, said he was running to the hardware store, and would return in a few minutes.

He sat on the edge of the chair across from me, forearms braced on his muscular thighs. Short black hair that held just a hint of gray at the temples was disheveled as though he'd run his fingers through it several times in agitation.

"I heard you earlier," he mumbled, no longer appearing aggressive. Now he just looked tired.

My mind went blank. "Heard me?" I echoed.

"Your conversation with Peggy. I left my wallet, so I dashed into the house to grab it and heard you and Peggy talking. I haven't been able to get the conversation out of my mind," he said in a much stronger voice.

I closed my eyes as realization struck. The voice I thought I'd heard. That had been Grant. Frantically, I thought back over the conversation, trying to remember exactly what I'd said and how much he might have heard. Licking my lips, I asked, "What did you hear?"

Grant's eyes narrowed and that little tick on his temple throbbed, showing his irritation. "Don't."

"Don't what?" I repeated, praying he'd drop the subject. I knew exactly what. Why the hell had I brought up the subject with Peggy?

He flattened his hands on his knees and leaned forward aggressively. "Don't deflect. Don't hide. Don't try to see how much I heard so you can judge how much to tell me. Take your pick."

I swallowed hard and glanced away from his intense stare. Nibbling my lower lip, I slowly sank back onto my seat as I berated myself. In my desperation to reconnect with Peggy, I'd blurted out something better kept to myself. Now look at the mess I'd created with my refusal to simply let go.

When I didn't respond, Grant continued, "You said, I've never had an orgasm. I'd like to know what you meant. Has sex with me been that unsatisfying?"

At that, my attention jerked back to my husband. Before I knew it, I'd moved. I rounded the table and straddled Grant's lap, cupping his jaw with my hand. "No, baby. Don't think that."

"How can I not?" he asked. Usually, in this position, Grant would grip me by the hips. I was acutely aware he made no attempt to touch me. His thighs felt like granite beneath my hips, revealing how tense he was.

"Because it's not true. This is why I didn't want to talk about it. I knew you'd blame yourself, and it's not your fault. You're a fantastic lover. I couldn't ask for better," I said, smoothing down his hair. I gazed directly into his eyes, hoping he'd read my sincerity.

Finally, Grant wrapped his arms around my hips and pulled me closer into a more lover-like embrace. "How do I know you aren't just saying that?"

Sighing, I rested my hands on his shoulders and kneaded the tight muscles. "Because it's the truth. Look, I love our sex life. Trust me when I say that the issue is me. I did a little research on the topic. Did you know that only thirty percent of women orgasm during sex with a partner?"

Grant frowned. "What are you saying?"

I rubbed my hands up and down his front, enjoying the feel of his broad chest. "I'm saying a woman failing to orgasm during sex is so common they have a name for it: Anorgasmia. Women either don't orgasm, orgasm infrequently, or have less-intense orgasms after being sexually aroused. I think I fall into the latter category."

Grant's gaze became even more intense and his grip tightened on my hips. "Why?"

Reminding myself that I could tell my husband anything, I took a deep breath and prepared to bare my soul. "I don't have a problem becoming aroused. As I said, I enjoy sex and you provide plenty of stimulation. I think my problem is that either I don't know how to let go and climax, or maybe I don't know what a climax is. There have been a few times..."

"Yes?" he asked when I trailed off.

I sighed and plucked at the front of his shirt. "There have been times while making love that I felt something so powerful that it freaked me out. I got scared and shut it down. Afterward, I felt empty as if I'd missed out on something really important. The research I've done makes me wonder if what I'd almost experienced was a climax."

Chapter Three

Grant

Sincerity radiated from Sasha's deep brown eyes. Her expression was so earnest, it made my chest ache. Hell, I didn't know what to think. She'd always seemed eager enough when we made love. My thoughts drifted back to last night…

"Aren't you coming to bed?" I asked.

Sasha looked up with a questioning glance from the couch where she reclined, reading on her tablet. "As soon as I finish this chapter."

"Are you sure you don't want to finish it later?" The look I'd given held all sorts of heat, suggesting that sleeping was not on my mind.

"Oh," she said, as understanding dawned. "Well, when you put it like that…"

I held out my hand in invitation, and she set her tablet on the coffee table. A sultry smile graced her plump lips as she accompanied me upstairs to our bedroom. We separated to perform our nightly bedtime rituals and came together again in bed.

Taking my time, I peppered kisses all over Sasha's beautiful body. I stroked her silken heat until my fingers were slick with her desire, her moans filled the room, and her body bowed with pleasure. Only when her nails dug into my shoulders and she demanded I come inside did I cease my sensuous torture and enter her. Seeking her pleasure first, I held off my release until I felt her sex ripple around me.

"Grant, honey, you believe me, don't you?" Sasha asked, interrupting my thoughts.

Had last night been a lie? Memories of other times we'd made love flashed through my mind. Had it all been a lie? I stared at her blankly, looking but not really seeing.

"Don't you, honey?" she asked.

Suddenly I focused on Sasha, realizing I'd lost the thread of the conversation and didn't have a clue what she'd asked. Her nails dug into my shoulders in silent demand and her tone conveyed concerned urgency. Patting her thigh in a reassuring manner, I said, "Of course. What's for dinner?"

Sasha's face scrunched into the picture of confusion. "Dinner? That's what you want to discuss? Now?"

What I wanted was out of this awkward conversation. I glanced into the kitchen. "I noticed you didn't take anything out."

"I forgot," she confessed. "Grant, we should really–"

"Tell you what," I said, speaking over her. "Why don't you put on something pretty, and we'll go to that Greek place you like. Maybe afterward, we'll walk along the river and get an ice cream cone from one of the street vendors. Let's make it a date."

"Sure, but..." Sasha stammered before bursting out, "Don't you want to talk?"

I shrugged, feigning nonchalance. "What's there to discuss? You said it wasn't me. That this is a female issue like periods, pregnancy, and menopause. I can be supportive, but there's nothing I can do to fix it, right? You'd tell me if I'm the problem?" I studied her closely, watching for any betraying twitch or flicker of her eyelashes that would confirm she'd softened the truth to spare my feelings.

Sasha nibbled her lower lip before hesitantly admitting, "I wouldn't have stated it like that, but it's a good analogy. Yes, this is a me issue. No, there's nothing you need to do except keep being your lovable, sexy self. If I think of anything you can do to assist me, I'll let you know." She leaned forward and gave me a lingering kiss. "Thank you for being understanding and willing to let me work through this issue on my own. I'd love to go on a date with you."

I didn't understand shit, but still I looked my sweet wife right in the eyes and nodded in agreement. "Want to go now? It's a bit early for dinner, but that means we'll beat the crowd," I suggested.

Sasha glanced at her watch, and I could see her mentally calculating. I'd arrived home after three. It should be close to four now. By the time we changed and drove to the restaurant, it would be almost five when we arrived.

"Yes, let's go now. I'd rather eat early than have a long wait," she agreed.

We walked upstairs. Just outside of our bedroom, I said, "You take our bathroom. I'll use the kids."

"All right," Sasha agreed, still sending me searching glances.

I grabbed a change of clothes and beat a hasty retreat. As I showered and dressed, my mind worried the problem like a terrier with a bone. Sasha claimed I wasn't the issue, but could I believe her? Sasha was tenderhearted. She wouldn't tell me I was a lousy lover. She'd said as much to Peggy.

Hell, every man thought he was good at sex–that was ego–but I'd worked at it to be sure. To master the art of foreplay, I'd read every sexual manual I could find written by women for men that explained what they wanted when it came to sex. Then I'd committed it to memory and made it a rule: the woman comes first. It was a point of honor. I'd put what I'd learned to practice while I was a randy college student. Now, with Sasha, the habit was ingrained. Didn't they say a satisfied wife meant a happy life?

Shaking my head, I brooded. If I was such an awesome lover, how in the hell had I missed for over twenty years that my wife hadn't orgasmed? Sasha had been right there with me every step of the way, or so I'd believed. How could I have been so wrong? So blind?

If she'd made this confession when the children were younger, I'd have understood. Foreplay took time, and often, time had been in short supply. Our days were long and we'd often been exhausted by bedtime. Also, there'd been the concern that one of the children would interrupt us right at a critical moment.

In addition, we had an open-door policy, which didn't allow for much privacy. However, we'd both agreed making our children feel loved and secure took priority over our sex life. Children stayed young for such a short period of time. It meant we'd had to forgo sleeping naked in favor of pajamas, and our lovemaking had been relegated to late-night or early-morning sexual encounters when we were sure the kids were asleep.

To compensate, each year for our anniversary, we'd arrange for either Sasha's parents or mine to watch the kids for a week. The children got to spend uninterrupted time with their grandparents, and Sasha and I got to reconnect as a couple. Those vacations turned into mini honeymoons where I'd made up for our lack of sexual intimacy during the rest of the year. Or, I'd tried. Hell, today's revelation had me reevaluating everything I thought I knew about our sex life.

A distressing thought crossed my mind. What if Sasha decided I couldn't satisfy her and went looking for someone who could? After all, how much of a loser did you have to be to not realize that your wife wasn't getting as much enjoyment from sex as you?

I shoved away those depressing thoughts and headed downstairs to wait for Sasha. Once we became empty nesters, I made reconnecting with Sasha my mission. Too many of my friends' and colleagues' marriages were falling apart. Our social circle had completely changed. I determined Sasha and I wouldn't follow down the same path.

I damned sure wouldn't be like Tom. He was the poster child for a midlife crisis. Tom and Peggy had been childhood sweethearts. The closer he'd gotten to forty, the more he'd begun to wonder what he'd missed out on by marrying so young. Once he started down that path, it hadn't been long before his dick had begun making his decisions. In the end, the stupid man had lost his financial status, embarrassed his family, and become the laughingstock of the people who knew him. The fool thought he was living his best life, but instead, he was a pathetic cliché.

I waited in the foyer, studying Sasha as she exited the staircase. Tom had wanted a younger model, claiming Peggy just didn't do it for him anymore. I had no reason to go looking elsewhere. Sasha was gorgeous, inside and out. She was one of those women who blossomed with age. Maturity had graced her with smile lines around her eyes and mouth, fuller hips, and a slightly rounded stomach, but otherwise, Sasha still looked the way she did when she was in her twenties.

From her Egyptian mother and Indian father, she'd inherited beautiful brown skin, deep brown eyes, a narrow nose, plump lips, and high cheekbones. She wore her coarse, black hair in a straight fall that landed just below her shoulder blades. Her full lips pressed together in a rare frown and worry made the fine lines around her eyes more prominent. "Are you sure you don't want to continue our discussion? It's not like you to just let a matter drop. You normally like to beat a subject into the ground until all I want to do is scream."

"Maybe I'm learning wisdom in my old age," I suggested lightly as we entered the garage.

Her "If you say so" sounded so dubious, I laughed and found my normally good humor restored.

As we drove to the restaurant, our conversation flowed as freely as always. No matter what else happened between us, Sasha and I had always been great friends. Our friendship had gotten us through several rough patches in our marriage. I only hoped it continued to do so.

A Taste of Greece was a slightly upscale, third-generation, family-owned and operated Greek restaurant. They specialized in Mediterranean cuisine, the food was fabulous, and the portions generous. On weekends, unless you called ahead as I had and reserved a seat, you could expect to wait upwards of an hour for a table.

We arrived and I gave our names to the hostess, who consulted her computer. "Your table will be ready in five minutes. Would you like something from the bar while you wait?"

I glanced at Sasha.

"I can wait until we're seated," Sasha said.

"We'll wait," I told the hostess.

"I'll call your name when your table is ready," the hostess said. As we turned to go to the waiting area, she smiled at the next person in line. "Welcome to *A Taste of Greece*. How many in your party?"

I settled my hand low on Sasha's back as we walked. The bench seats in the alcove were taken so we stood off to the side out of the main walkway. Sasha studied the pictures on the wall. I watched the men checking out my wife, frowning when I caught one staring at her ass. I stepped in front of her, blocking his view. When he glanced up, I glared my displeasure. The man gave a rueful smile and turned his attention back to his companion.

As always, my wife was sexy as hell. Tonight, she wore a dress with a rounded collar that circled her neck like a necklace and left her toned arms and shoulders bare. The colorful dress fit snug over full breasts and skimmed her curvy body, stopping just above the knee. She'd left her thick, black hair loose. The heeled sandals highlight pedicured feet and shapely calves.

The avid staring continued as we were escorted to our table. The male servers were attentive and flirty, blatantly ignoring the huge rock on my wife's left hand. For Sasha's sake, I tamped down my irritation. Men hit on her wherever we went. It annoyed me, but Sasha was oblivious. If I mentioned it, she'd only laugh it off, not believing a word I said. How long before she stopped laughing and started paying attention?

Despite the crowd, the service was swift. Another reason we enjoyed dining here. Sasha had the orange roasted lamb, potatoes, and a Greek salad as an appetizer. I ordered the lamb souvlaki, which was chunks of lamb grilled on a skewer and grilled potatoes, served with tzatziki sauce. Other than the occasional glass of wine, neither of us was a big drinker, so we ordered sweet tea with our meal.

Our small talk continued throughout dinner. Then our conversation shifted to the kids.

"You think she's okay?" Sasha asked.

I fought the urge to roll my eyes. "Honey, it's only been a little over a month. She's fine. If not, she knows how to pick up the phone and call.

Sasha sighed. "I know you think I'm silly for worrying. It's just that of the two of them, Wendi's always been a little flighty."

This had been Sasha's reasoning for wanting Wendi to attend a local college, at least for the first two years as she earned her Associate of Arts degree. She worried Wendi was too immature to be on her own. I'd been of the opinion that living on campus was a good transition. Her school was only three hours away, and it would force our sheltered daughter to take responsibility for herself and grow up.

"Wendi will never mature if we keep coddling her," I said.

Our daughter had the brains of a computer but the attention span of a flea, unless the subject interested her. She'd lost cell phones, countless house keys, and her wallet twice. When she turned sixteen, I'd taught Wendi how to drive but refused to let her get her driver's license until she proved she could keep her attention on the road. I still worried she'd crash her car one day because she was distracted by her phone. I understood Sasha's concern.

"I wish someone had warned me parenting would be so hard," she said.

I reached out and captured her hand, holding it in mine. "You did a fantastic job raising them. It's time to let them spread their wings and fly, momma bird. I promise you, if they fall, you can swoop in and catch them."

Sasha gave me a rueful smile. "Okay, daddy bird. I'll stop worrying."

"No, you won't, but it's okay. That's what I'm here for. Are you finished?" I asked.

Sasha looked at her half-full plate. "I can't eat another bite."

"I'll ask the server for to-go boxes."

Sasha planted her elbows on the table and propped her chin on her hands. "I'm glad we did this. It reminds me of how things used to be before we had kids."

"We've spent enough time being parents. It's time to get back to us," I said as the server approached with the check.

"I agree," she murmured.

I paid for the meal, leaving the server a generous tip, and escorted Sasha out of the restaurant.

"Did you save room for ice cream?" I asked as I held open the passenger car door.

She rubbed her stomach. "I'm full. Maybe after we walk off some of this food, I'll have room."

"Tuck in," I said. Sasha slid into the car, swung her feet around, and made sure her dress wouldn't get caught in the door. Leaning in, I lightly kissed her lips before carefully closing the door and striding around to the driver's side.

Chapter Four

Sasha

On the drive home, I floated in a romantic haze. The early eighties radio station played our favorite makeout songs when Grant and I were dating. Despite the rocky start, the evening had been absolutely amazing. Grant had been super attentive. He hadn't looked at his phone once. There had been no interruptions. No "Give me a second to respond to this email" or "Hold on for a minute while I check the market." My soul feasted on every second.

Even now, with his arm resting on the center console, Grant held my hand in his. Occasionally he'd rub the back of my hand with his thumb or toy with my wedding ring. I glanced at our joined hands, seeing the ring sparkle in the passing streetlights. For our twentieth anniversary, Grant had gifted me with a three-carat eternity band that matched my wedding set perfectly. I loved him so much. I felt sorry for women who didn't have a Grant in their lives.

Grant parked the car in the driveway, and I waited for him to come open my door. As I exited the vehicle, he leaned forward and gave me a lingering kiss. "Thank you for a wonderful night."

"No, thank you. We should do this more often," I said with a happy sigh.

"We will," he promised.

We walked hand-in-hand up the walkway. As I waited for Grant to unlock the door and punch in the security code to the alarm, anticipation thrummed in my veins. A night like this could only end one way. "I'm going to go up and get ready for bed," I tossed over my shoulder, adding an extra sway in my hips as I walked towards the stairs.

"Be up in a minute. I just need to lock up and set the alarm," Grant said.

There was a bounce in my step as I almost jogged up the stairs. Seconds later, I'd hung my dress in the closet and stood in our bathroom in my strapless bra and matching panties, washing the makeup from my face. After applying moisturizer and brushing my teeth, I sauntered into the bedroom. Grant still hadn't arrived, so I put on a sexy babydoll.

The spaghetti straps left my arms bare. A deep V-neck exposed a nice amount of cleavage, and the lace cups hugged my breasts. The satiny, jade-green material flattered my complexion, and the gathered skirt camouflaged my belly. It stopped at mid-thigh, showing off my long legs. Wearing it made me feel desirable and sexy. Sitting on the bed, I lotioned my arms and legs with a scented body cream that left my skin silky smooth. Then I waited. And waited.

Arousal gradually turned to curiosity. What was taking Grant so long? It had been a little after ten when we walked into the house. It was now edging toward eleven. Climbing off the queen-sized bed, I put on my robe and slippers and headed downstairs. As I neared the bottom of the staircase, I could hear the low volume of the television in the den. What the hell?

Most of the lights on the lower level were off and only the glow of the sixty-five-inch flat-screen television in the den and the hallway light upstairs lit the way. I walked into the semi-darkness of the den and found Grant reclined in his favorite black leather recliner. A bottle of water sat on the table near his side.

"I thought you were coming up?" I said.

Grant glanced over, and his eyes quickly skimmed my body. "I am. I just want to check the stock market first. You don't have to wait up. It's been a long day."

I stared blankly. The commercial ended, and Grant's attention returned to the scrolling numbers on the screen. After long minutes of waiting for Grant to tell me this was a joke, I finally mumbled, "Good night."

He threw up a hand, telling me bye, but his gaze never left the television.

I slowly turned and walked up the stairs, my mind a mass of confusion. What just happened? Not once had Grant ever missed any of my signals that I wanted sex. I thought back over my actions. Had I not been clear enough?

Our after dinner stroll had been full of loving touches and lingering kisses. I'd responded eagerly to his kiss when we arrived home, pressing my body against his in invitation. I'd felt his erection and knew he was aroused. Husky voice, come hither eyes, and sexy sway to my hips? Message sent and received. Grant was supposed to come up and find me waiting in bed. He'd undress, and we'd make love. That was our pattern.

I took off my robe and tossed it over my reading chair. After placing my bedroom shoes where I could easily slide into them in the morning, I climbed into bed. My mind raced, puzzling out the situation. I came to the only conclusion available to me. Grant was more upset about our conversation than he'd let on.

Briefly, I debated going downstairs to confront him but changed my mind as soon as the thought occurred. I'd known there was a problem when he dropped the subject. That wasn't Grant's way. Pushing the issue now might do more harm than good. Grant hadn't asked questions. Even if he had, I didn't have answers other than what I'd already shared. Assuring him this was my issue, not his, obviously hadn't done the trick.

I honestly didn't know what to do. Maybe I should just give it time and hope things worked themselves out. Turning onto my side, I plumped my pillow and prayed I hadn't ruined our nearly perfect marriage with my confession.

Weeks later, our sex life was on life support. We normally had sex two-to-three times a week. Now we had none. Our sex life hadn't gradually dwindled. It had abruptly ceased, and I was at my wits' end.

All of my subtle hints for sex were ignored. I was afraid to be more direct with my desire lest I be rebuffed. When I tentatively brought up the subject, Grant pretended not to know what I was talking about. He was still as affectionate as ever, but whenever I tried to take things to the next level, Grant pulled back.

When I finally managed to corner him, he'd stated patiently, "I'm giving you time to work on your issue." I'd had no argument since I was the one who told him there was nothing he could do to help.

Other than our sex life, things had never been better. We went on dates a couple of times a week. On workdays, he called or texted every day at lunch to connect. We spent our evenings watching television or reading companionably. As long as the discussion wasn't about sex, conversations flowed as freely as ever.

The minute night fell and it was time to go to bed, the atmosphere changed. Grant found excuses not to come upstairs until after he thought I was asleep. If he came and I was still awake, I pretended to be asleep. I wasn't sure how much longer I could continue like this.

✧ ✧ ✧ ✧ ✧

My stomach rolled like I'd eaten something sour. Dread and nerves had me on the verge of throwing up. Today was the day. I paced the den, waiting to hear Grant's car pull into the garage. Dinner waited on the stove, and I'd set the table on the back patio. Tonight, I would push past my discomfort and bring everything out into the open. As much as I hated confrontations, my gut told me it was necessary if I wanted to save my marriage.

I heard the garage door opening and took a deep, steadying breath. I could do this. I had to do this. Wiping damp palms on my thighs, I examined my appearance in the foyer's decorative wall mirror. I'd put on my favorite sundress. The bohemian print, halter-style dress toed the line between dressy and casual. I'd pulled my hair into a simple ponytail. If I dismissed the stress lines around my eyes and the tightness of my mouth, I looked good.

For dinner, I'd prepared Grant's favorite meal: creamy lemon chicken piccata, Caesar salad, and for dessert, an easy lemon pound cake recipe I'd found online. I scurried into the kitchen and hovered near the island, wringing my hands, on the verge of panicking. Was it too obvious? Was I trying too hard?

The inner door leading to the garage closed and seconds later, Grant entered the kitchen. He'd loosened his tie in the car and had his suit jacket slung casually over one shoulder. He set his briefcase on the floor and gave me a quick kiss before inhaling deeply. "Something smells good."

"Lemon piccata. Why don't you go upstairs and change out of those work clothes? The weather's nice, not too hot, and the breeze is lovely. I thought we could enjoy our meal on the patio while looking out over the lake," I said, hoping my voice didn't tremble.

Grant cast me a wary glance. "My favorite, and I smell cake. Are we celebrating something? I didn't forget our anniversary, did I?"

I rolled my eyes. "Our wedding anniversary isn't for another month."

"The anniversary of our first date? First kiss? The first time we made love?" He quirked an eyebrow but the twinkle in his eyes said he was teasing.

"No, silly." Laughing felt good and eased some of my inner tension. "Go change. I'll plate the food and carry it outside."

He turned and headed upstairs. I quickly filled two plates, giving Grant a much larger portion, and took them to the table. Grant met me as I carried the glasses of iced tea. "Grab the salads, will you?" I asked, motioning with my head towards the countertop.

"Which salad dressing do you want?" he asked.

"Ranch, please."

Grant shook his head. "Who eats ranch dressing on a Caesar salad?"

"I do." I disliked Caesar dressing. Grant disliked ranch, which I found incomprehensible.

"This looks good. Thank you," Grant said as we sat at the table.

He reached for his fork and dug in with gusto. I pushed food around on my plate, taking small bites here and there. My stomach was so knotted I couldn't force myself to eat. Grant talked and I listened, adding the occasional comment or noise to show I was engaged.

The minute he finished his last bite of food, I stood and reached for his plate. "I'll take our plates into the kitchen," I said, hoping Grant wouldn't notice that I'd barely eaten.

"I'll help," Grant said, rising to assist.

I waved him away. "Sit. Relax. I'm just going to put these in the sink and bring out the cake."

He studied my face closely. Knowing me as well as he did, I was pretty sure he saw how jittery I was, though I tried to hide it. "Okay."

That Grant didn't ask me what was wrong showed just how far down the rabbit hole we'd fallen. I scraped the food residue into the trash and placed the plates in the dishwasher for later. Then with hands that noticeably trembled, I cut two slices of cake and plated them. After taking another steadying breath, I returned to the patio with two cake slices, two wine glasses, and a bottle of Rosé.

Grant eyed the wine. "Is what you have to say so bad I need alcohol to handle it?"

"The wine is for me. I'm allowing you to share," I said, trying to tease but coming off flat.

"I think I'd rather hear what you have to say," he said, pushing his cake to the side.

I took a large swallow of wine, knowing it was now or never. Remembering the advice of my counselor, I made "I" statements, keeping the focus on me. "I miss us. We talk, but it feels like there's a wall between us. I can't complain because it's totally my fault."

I paused to take another sip of wine, giving Grant a chance to speak and tell me I was wrong. He said nothing. Just watched me with careful eyes. I swallowed more wine and reminded myself I'd known this would be hard. Grant might be the "let's face this head-on and get it settled" type about most issues, but when his feelings were hurt or his ego bruised, he was as silent and broody as any male.

"I owe you an apology. A couple, in fact," I admitted.

Grant leaned back in his seat and crossed his arms over his chest. "For?" he asked, as straight-faced and remote as ever.

He wasn't making this easy for me, but then, I hadn't expected him to do so. "First, our sex life is private. I should have never discussed it with Peggy, or anyone else. Even if..." No, no excuses. Stick to the facts. "I shouldn't have done it. Had our roles been reversed, I'd be livid. I am truly sorry, and I promise I'll work hard not to let it happen again."

With Peggy no longer in my life, it truly wouldn't happen again, but I didn't want to go into details now about my ruined friendship.

Grant was silent as he digested my apology. I didn't push for a response. Apologizing was my responsibility. It was up to him to accept it or not.

"All right," he said.

I wanted more, but I'd created this monster issue so I couldn't complain. Continuing with my apology, I said, "I've been seeing an online therapist for a few weeks now."

"You contacted a therapist?" Grant interrupted, his brows lowered in a frown.

"Yes, I told you that this was a me issue. That leads me to apology number two. Anita Frazier, my therapist, helped me to see that any issue involving sex is never simply my problem alone. What happens with me affects you, too. I was wrong to exclude you. If the offer is still open, I'm asking for help," I said, holding my breath.

Grant leaned forward and braced his elbows on the table, pinning me with a stony stare. I could feel the waves of anger radiating from him. "Why didn't you tell me you were in therapy? Don't you think that's something I'd want to know?"

I shrank back in my seat. "Whenever I brought up the subject of sex, you blew me off." It's not like I hadn't tried to talk with him about it. Maybe I hadn't pushed, but I'd brought it up.

"Sasha, it's not that hard. You simply say, 'Grant, I'm seeing a therapist.' That's different from talking about our sex life," he said.

"How is that different?" I asked, truly bewildered.

He shoved to his feet and clasped a hand to the back of his head. "I didn't want to discuss sex because I thought you were going to blame me," he said.

Voice rising, I gripped the table in front of me to stay in my seat. "Why would I do that? I've stated from the beginning that you weren't the problem."

Grant planted his hands on his waist. "It's what you said but was it the truth? Everyone knows if the woman can't climax with a man, it's the man's fault," he argued.

I slowly pushed to my feet and faced off with him across the table. My slow-to-burn anger had finally come out to play. "Grant, that's pure bullshit. According to the books I've been reading, I'm responsible for my pleasure, not you."

He reared back, eyes widening in shock. "What the hell does that mean?"

"It means I have a mouth, and I haven't been using it." The finger I pointed at him shook as I continued. "You're a great lover, Grant, and that's part of the problem. You always seem to know what will make me feel good, and you're an expert at reading my body language. Because of it, I just went with the flow, following wherever you led, and that's wrong on so many levels." My words exploded like detonating bombs.

We stared at each other for long, charged-filled minutes.

Finally, in a much quieter voice, Grant asked, "What's wrong with that? I love pleasuring you."

As though he'd released a pressure valve, the tension in the room dissipated. My rapidly beating heart slowed, and I exhaled deeply to release the last of my agitation. I wanted to touch Grant, to reassure myself of our connection, but now was not the time. We were finally getting to the heart of the matter.

I rubbed a hand over my heart in an attempt to soothe the ache there before saying, "I know, honey, and I love that you do. Let me ask you a question, and please answer honestly. Does it ever bother you that I don't express my needs, or that the majority of the time, you're the one who has to initiate sex?"

Grant visibly hesitated, returned to his seat, and slowly lowered into it. It felt like he was giving himself time before answering. I sat across from him and waited for his response, my leg bouncing unseen beneath the table.

"Maybe at the beginning when we were first married, but I get that it's not how you're wired. You're not the demanding sort," he said with a shrug. "As for initiating sex, you do your fair share, and you rarely turn me down when I do, so it's all good."

I stopped bouncing my leg and glanced down at my clasped hands, sighing inwardly. "No, it's really not. Doing so puts the pressure and responsibility of my pleasure on you and that's not how it's supposed to be. We're a team. Sexual honesty is a form of trust, and by not expressing myself, I've let both of us down."

Grant reclined in his chair, but his gaze was observant. "You learned all of that from a book?"

My smile was rueful. "Sort of. My therapist brought it to my attention first, and the books reinforced it. If you're interested in what I've been learning, I can share my self-help books with you. They're written by a sex therapist. I'm not saying you need them," I rushed to add, "but reading them might give you a better understanding of my issues." In no way did I want Grant to continue thinking he was the problem.

He made a noncommittal sound. "Maybe one day I'll read it."

I sighed in relief. Our troubles weren't over, but I believed we were over the biggest hurdle. We were communicating. As long as we could discuss it, there was no issue we couldn't overcome.

Chapter Five

Grant

Sasha's temper was like lighting a fire with damp wood. It was slow to ignite, easy to extinguish, but smoked for a long time. Sasha reached for her wine glass, drew her feet under, and curled into the chair in a relaxed pose, but I could see remnants of tension around her eyes. She was still on edge but trying to hide it.

My wife was seeing a therapist for her sex issues. I thought she'd do as Peggy suggested–masturbate until she figured out what got her off. Then we'd return to having regular sex where I'd continue to fuck up because Sasha wouldn't share what I was doing wrong. After the sex was over, she'd wait until I was asleep or until she was alone in the bathroom and give herself the fulfillment I hadn't. Her bringing a therapist into the picture changed my perspective. Was it possible she'd been stating the truth?

A sudden thought occurred and left a sour taste in my mouth. I picked up my wine glass and tossed back half the contents, wishing it were whiskey. "Sasha," I said very carefully, "were you the victim of sexual assault? If you were, you know you can talk with me about it, right?"

Sasha appeared blank. "What? No. Where'd you get an idea like that?"

Not sure I believed her, I gently said, "You're seeing a sex therapist. They help people who've suffered sexual abuse in their childhood or as an adult."

The soft smile she gave me was filled with understanding. "Grant, they also help individuals and couples who, for whatever reason, have difficulty with sex or simply want a more intimate sexual experience. On the surface, sex sounds easy. Slide tab A into slot B and move it around until everyone is satisfied, but what happens if one or both partners are dissatisfied? What happens when one partner wants things the other can't or won't provide? What happens if the sex you used to have is no longer an option because of illness, an accident, or aging? A qualified sex therapist helps couples navigate all of these issues. Wait just a second."

Sasha jumped up and hurried into the house, leaving me reeling. Before overhearing her and Peggy's conversation, I would have scoffed at the idea of bringing a so-called sex expert into our relationship. What we had was just fine and any issues that arose, we'd handle it ourselves. I had a feeling that before today was over, Sasha would force me to reconsider my position.

She returned with a book tucked under her arm. Setting the book on the table, Sasha topped off her glass of wine and held up the bottle. "Would you like more?"

I held out my glass. Before this painful discussion ended, we'd probably both be hammered.

Sasha filled mine to the rim and placed the bottle on the table. Once she was seated, she grabbed the book and held it up so I could read the cover. "This is one of the books I mentioned. Of them all, I liked this one the best."

I read the title, **Sex without Stress**, and looked at my wife. Was she sending me a coded message? Did she find our sex life stressful? Had I fucked up that badly? I raised my glass and took a large swallow.

"I told you I've learned a great deal from this book. Dr. Zimmerman opens the book with case studies made-up of imaginary couples to give examples of reasons why a couple might seek therapy. One of them really caught my attention. I grabbed the book because I didn't want to get the details wrong," she said. As she sat, Sasha opened the book and began flipping pages.

I wasn't sure I wanted to hear anything this book had to say.

Sasha made a soft humming sound when she reached the correct page. "As I stated, this couple hit home because this could be us in another fifteen to twenty years."

I barely held back a snort. There was no way.

She skimmed a finger along the passage as she refreshed her memory. "They're best friends, have a great marriage, and had an active sex life until the husband began suffering from erectile dysfunction." I winced and barely resisted the urge to protectively cup my balls. "He takes Viagra, but sometimes it doesn't work. Where before thinking about or anticipating sex was enough to get him hard, now he needs physical stimulation. His condition embarrasses him, so he hasn't discussed it with his wife. As a result, she thinks he no longer finds her physically attractive."

Caught up in the story, I said, "That's stupid. There's no way I'd ever stop wanting you, no matter how old we get."

Sasha shook her head. "The wife unknowingly gauges her desirability by how her husband responds to her sexually. In addition, she survived breast cancer but had to have a double mastectomy. Her breasts were very sensitive and a source of great pleasure. Now all she has is scar tissue where her breasts should be. Losing her breasts left her even more uncertain about her femininity–"

"And because her husband can't get it up, she thinks it's because her breasts are gone," I said, seeing where Sasha was going with this.

Sasha jabbed a finger at me and grinned. "Yes, exactly! Their sex life was something they just did but never discussed. Now, he's scared to touch her because he doesn't want to hurt her and doesn't know how she feels about her body after the mastectomy. Even if he brought it up, she couldn't tell him because she hasn't let herself think about it too closely. Another problem is that he's always been the one to initiate sex. As if they don't have enough problems, she finds the act of touching his penis unnecessary and distasteful. I don't remember if the author said it was her upbringing or religious background," Sasha said, scanning the page.

A brief frown formed as I wondered if Sasha felt the same. Not ready to broach that subject, I said instead, "I thought you said they were best friends? Why don't they just sit down and confront the issue?" I asked, the solution obvious to me.

"He blames himself, and she blames herself and him, too. They each think the other no longer finds them sexually desirable, and they're scared to have their suspicions confirmed. Dr. Zimmerman said a person's sexual image is very personal and tied to their identity. It takes a tremendous amount of trust to be open and vulnerable with a person because with a few careless words, they can destroy your self-image," she finished thoughtfully.

Sasha's words hit me where it hurt. Wasn't that why I'd recently avoided all conversations about sex? Her revelation challenged my perception of myself as a lover. Despite her protestations, I blamed myself for her inability to orgasm. I took a bite of cake to keep from speaking. A blind man could see the parallel between them and us.

A nice breeze came through the window. Ducks on the pond quacked as they sought their evening meal. I could hear neighbors moving around in their yards and cars driving by on the street. The sun turned an orangish glow as it slowly sank in the west.

"How's the cake?" Sasha asked, watching me closely.

"What?" I asked blankly.

"The cake. Do you like it? It's a new recipe. Only five ingredients. It's the easiest pound cake I've ever made," she said.

I looked down at the dessert plate in my hand. I'd eaten over half the slice she'd given me and hadn't tasted a thing. I broke off another piece and placed it in my mouth, really tasting it this time. "It's good. Moist. Is that lemon I taste?"

"Yes. I put lemon extract in it. The recipe didn't call for it, but I thought it would give it a nice touch." There was a brief pause before

Sasha continued in a rush, "Annie, my therapist, wants you to join one of my sessions. She said counseling works best when both partners are present."

"No."

Sasha slow-blinked, as though she couldn't believe my response. "No? I thought you wanted to help?"

"No," I repeated. "I'll help you in any other way but that."

She lowered her eyes and flipped the corner pages of the book in her lap.

"Sasha." I waited until she looked at me. "You know how I feel about therapy. I let you drag me to a marriage counselor once, against my better judgment, and the man was a quack. He almost destroyed our marriage. We paid his outrageous fee only to work out the issue ourselves. I told you then, never again."

"But Annie's different. She comes highly recommended, and her reviews are fantastic. I think you'll like her," Sasha said, her eyes pleading.

"No," I said again, my response simple but firm.

Sighing, Sasha pushed the book aside and picked up her wine glass. "I knew it was a long shot, but I had to ask."

"If you want to share what's said in your sessions with me or read me things from that book you find fascinating, I'm open to it," I said, feeling guilty but knowing this was a line I wouldn't cross. Weren't therapists all about boundaries? Well, this was mine.

"Thank you." Sasha picked up her fork and began eating her cake.

I felt like shit. Sasha looked like a kicked puppy. I, more than anyone, knew how hard confronting me had been. I scrambled for something to say. "I don't understand what benefit it serves for me to attend. You said I wasn't the problem."

No, damn it. That wasn't what I meant to say, though it was uppermost in my thoughts. I didn't want to give Sasha hope that I might change my mind.

"She said most couples' disappointment with sex comes from unmet expectations," Sasha said, perking up at my interest.

I didn't want to engage in further conversation on the subject. Unfortunately, her comment had tweaked my interest. "What does that mean?"

"She said everyone enters sex with some type of expectation. This example might be extreme, but it's the best way I can think of to explain what she meant. If you watch porn, you might expect all of your sexual encounters to be like what you see on screen, not realizing it's staged and not real life. In my case, I was completely satisfied with our sex life until I read that romance novel–"

"You wanted me to act like the hero in the book?" I said, my tone showing my horror at the idea. Did I need to read the damn book? Use it as a how-to guide?

"No, that's not what I want at all," she said, her tone rising. Sasha frowned and shook her head, her expression one of extreme frustration. "It was the description of the heroine's orgasm that triggered a memory and helped me put a name to what I'd felt. I didn't realize that the sensation I told you about was building to a powerful orgasm before I squashed it. Reading the book, realizing what I'd experienced was real and not something I made up, caused me to wonder what I'd been missing out on because of fear."

Damn if her explanation didn't make sense. I sighed and wearily ran my finger through my hair, giving my emotions a minute to settle. I needed to stop being so damned touchy. No matter how many times Sasha reassured me, I kept defaulting back to the idea that this situation was all my fault. Remembering what she'd said, I asked, "Before the book, what were your sexual expectations?"

Sasha leaned forward, her expression intent. "Exactly what you gave me–pleasure and connection. I love making love with you. Some of our most intimate moments are after sex. The way you hold me afterward and our conversations in the dark–I love all of it."

Sighing, I sagged in my chair and placed the back of my hand on my forehead. "Sasha, honey, if that were true, you wouldn't be in therapy."

My wife seemed to crumple, and I caught the glint of tears before she buried her face in her hands. "I don't know what to do or say to convince you," she sobbed. "Nothing I say seems to matter. You won't come to therapy with me so Anne can explain. God, I wish I'd never let Peggy talk me into reading that stupid book."

The sight of my wife's tears broke me. I couldn't take being apart from Sasha any longer. I jumped to my feet, quickly rounded the table and pulled her from her chair. "Don't cry. You know I hate it when you cry."

She collapsed against me. "You won't talk to me. You won't make love. I'm losing you and I don't know what to do about it."

I scooped her up into my arms and carried her to the couch, settling with her on my lap. "I'm such an ass. Don't cry, sweetheart. I'm sorry. Please forgive me."

Sasha wrapped her arms around my neck and cried out her pain and misery. I'd done this to her, me and my stupid ego. Instead of manning up, I'd wallowed in my hurt pride. "Shh, I'm sorry. We'll fix this. Whatever it takes, I'll make it up to you."

◇ ◇ ◇ ◇ ◇

We sat on the couch facing Sasha's laptop, which was situated on the coffee table. On the monitor was an older, African-American woman. I'd expected a staid professional. What I saw was a dark-skinned woman with multi-colored, neatly styled dreadlocks and a gold hoop nose ring. She wore stylish black framed glasses over intelligent brown eyes. The sleeveless, vest-like black top was the height of professionalism, but the tattoo sleeve on her left arm was not. The dichotomy of professional and bohemian left me disarmed and off-balanced.

"Sasha, good to see you again," Annie said in a voice laced with a light, lyrical Caribbean accent.

"Annie, thanks for meeting with us on a Saturday. This is my husband, Grant," Sasha said.

I nodded my head politely in greeting. No need inflicting my sour mood on anyone.

"Nice to meet you, Grant. Thank you for joining us," Annie said.

"I'm not here as a client," I said to be sure there was no misunderstanding my intent. "My wife asked me to meet you, and I agreed to one session."

Annie blinked. "I see. Sex therapy is more effective when both clients attend the sessions."

"That's not an option," I said. I knew Sasha hoped that this meeting with Annie would turn into something more. I was making clear that it wouldn't.

Annie didn't waste time trying to change my mind but jumped right into her session. "Sasha, would you like to discuss how your talk went with Grant?"

Sasha shifted in her seat next to me and wrung her hands in her lap. She flicked a glance at me before responding, "He doesn't believe me."

"What doesn't Grant believe?" Annie asked.

"He thinks my inability to orgasm is an indictment against him. Nothing I say can convince him otherwise," Sasha said in a rush.

"Grant?"

I felt called out somehow. "It's not that I don't believe her, per se," I hedged. "I know my wife. If she thought it would spare my feelings, she'd stretch the truth." I could feel Sasha staring at me.

"What I hear you saying is that you believe Sasha would lie if it would spare your feelings?" Annie asked.

"Yes," I answered.

"See?" Sasha said, throwing up her hands. "I even told him what you said about me being responsible for my pleasure, and that my lack of orgasm has nothing to do with his sexual prowess or lack thereof."

Annie leaned forward in her seat, her expression intent. "Grant, do you agree with Sasha's assessment of the situation?"

"It's a man's job to pleasure his woman," I said, still not looking directly at my wife.

"And by pleasure you mean...?" Annie asked.

"Help her to climax," I said.

"And if Sasha doesn't climax?" Annie asked.

"Then what's the point?" I asked with a shrug.

Sasha rounded on me. "That's why we haven't had sex?"

I slid a sideways glance at the monitor where Annie watched our interaction. "Can we discuss this later?"

"I want to talk about it now. Nothing I say seems to get through to you. Maybe Annie can help," Sasha said with a stubborn tilt to her chin and a determined glint in her eyes.

I turned to face my wife, mouth tightening with irritation. "Fine, you want to talk about this now? We'll talk. We haven't had sex because if you're not getting the same enjoyment out of it as me, then the whole thing is a waste of time."

Before an argument could ensue, Annie interjected, "So Grant, what you're saying is that the ultimate goal of sex is climaxing and without it, sex is pointless?"

"Yes."

"Sasha, your response to Grant is...?"

"Sex is about more than the orgasm. It's about intimacy and connection," Sasha argued. Her face held a dull flush that showed more than words that she was just as riled as I was.

"Bullshit. If intimacy and connection were all you wanted from sex, you wouldn't have sought out a sex therapist," I said.

The silence in the room was loud following my explosion.

Sasha's lower lip quivered, but she quickly firmed it. In a quiet voice she said, "I didn't say that it was all I wanted. I'm saying that for me there's more to sex than the big finish."

I stood, rounded the couch, and walked over to the sliding glass doors to look out over the lake.

"Just because I want to try for more doesn't mean I don't love what we have now. Our sex life doesn't have to be all or nothing. I don't see why that's so hard to understand," Sasha finished in the same quiet voice.

"Because it doesn't make sense," I said, not turning to face her.

In the window's reflection, I watched Sasha bite her lip as her gaze turned inward. "Let me put this in terms you'll understand."

"Please do," I said, turning to face her.

"Say I have a basic will and testament, and it satisfies all of my needs. Then I overhear someone talking about their irrevocable trust and how it's so much better than just a basic will and testament. My will got the job done, and I was happy with it, but now that I know there's something better, I'm curious."

Pushing past my ego and hurt, I analyzed her statement and for the first time, really heard what my wife was saying. "It's not that you're dissatisfied with our current love life. You wonder if there's something you're missing."

She gave me a beautiful smile. "Yes, that's exactly what I'm saying."

For the first time in weeks, the tension left my shoulders, and the sick feeling in my gut disappeared. I still had some mental readjusting to do to get the truth firmly settled in my mind, but I was finally on the right track.

I returned to my seat and took Sasha's hand in mine. "I'm sorry I was such a dick about this. My offer to help still stands. I won't attend sessions with you," I told Sasha before she could get her hopes up, "but I'll help in any other way." Turning to Annie, I said, "No offense, but that's one line I won't cross."

"No offense taken," Annie said.

Sasha turned to Annie. "What happens now?"

"Our time today is up, but in our next session, I can give you and Grant a few exercises I normally recommend to increase intimacy between couples," Annie said.

"I'd like that," Sasha said. "Grant?"

"You're in charge. I'll follow your lead," I said.

Sasha leaned her head on my shoulder. "It sounds like we have a plan."

Chapter Six

Grant

"Is everything okay?" Sasha asked as we ate dinner.

After the therapy session, I'd disappeared into my office and stayed there all day. "It's fine."

Sasha studied me. "I'm sorry for putting you on the spot earlier. I was afraid if we didn't talk about it then, we never would."

"It's fine," I said.

Sasha's face scrunched, half-amused, half-concerned. "That sounds like something I'd say."

With a heavy sigh, I set down my fork. "I'm processing, okay?"

She placed her hand on my arm and gave it a gentle squeeze. "That's what I do after speaking with Annie. She often gives me plenty to think about. I'll let you brood in peace."

The word brood made me sound like a moody asshole, but I'd take it if it meant she gave me much-needed space. My brain needed time to convince my emotions that this thing with Sasha really was her issue. Feelings of inadequacy and shame had grown, resulting in a mild case of erectile dysfunction. My mind knew the truth, but my body needed time to get on the same page.

The physical consequence of Sasha's confession wasn't something I wanted to discuss. One, it was embarrassing. Two, I didn't trust her to keep it between us, and three, Sasha would use it as an excuse to pressure me into joining her in therapy. I wasn't having it.

The rest of the weekend passed with me waiting for my body and brain to get on the same page. I stopped avoiding Sasha in bed. We didn't have sex, but I ramped up the physical affection. I owed it to her after the past few weeks. By Tuesday, I thought sex might soon be a possibility. On Wednesday, I came home from work, my body revving with anticipation. For the first time in ages, thoughts of making love to my wife didn't fill me with self-doubt and anxiety. Maybe, just maybe, I wouldn't choke when the moment arrived.

My first clue that my wife was up to something came when I walked into the house. The scents of garlic and marinara sauce filled the house. It smelled like my mom's lasagna. Sasha had prepared another one of my favorite meals.

Instantly wary, I dropped my briefcase and suit jacket in my office before strolling into the main part of the house. I stood in the kitchen's archway, frowning as I examined the scene. "What do you want?"

Sasha gave a nervous laugh. "Hello to you, too. How was your day?"

"The same as it was when we spoke at lunch. What's all this?" My hand motion took in the romantically set table and pan of lasagna resting on the stovetop. Sasha rarely made it, citing that the recipe was too much work.

She wore a flowy sundress that left her calves and a portion of her thighs bare. Her hair lay loose around her shoulders, the way I liked it. Her makeup was subtle but there. Sasha didn't wear makeup at home.

"Can't a wife do something nice for her husband without him being suspicious?" she asked in a teasing tone.

I brushed her smiling lips with a greeting kiss and placed my hands on her waist. "Yes, but we both know that's not what this is. Tell me what you want so we can enjoy the rest of our evening in peace."

Sasha nibbled her lower lip before sighing. "Annie gave me my homework assignment."

"And?" I'd already promised to assist her with it.

She took a deep breath and blurted, "She says I need to work on asking for what I want sexually. That it's not fair to you for me to expect you to just know. That I need to work on being an active participant."

The more she spoke, the deeper my frown grew. "She makes it sound like you just lay there and take it. What have you been telling this woman? That's not our sex life, at all."

Sasha pulled away from me and grimaced. "I'm making a mess of things. Let's sit, and I'll try to explain."

I followed her to the couch and dropped down beside her. Sasha brought her knee up on the cushion and turned to face me. I rested my arm along the back of the sofa and shifted towards her, giving her my full attention.

"Speaking with Annie made me realize that while I'm assertive in other areas of our relationship, when it comes to sex, I'm very passive. I follow where you lead, and while there's nothing wrong with that, it unfairly puts the responsibility for my pleasure on your shoulders."

"And that's a problem, why?" I liked being responsible for Sasha's pleasure, except... Thinking of these last few weeks, maybe Annie had a point. Being responsible for Sasha's pleasure also made me responsible for her dissatisfaction, right? Something I still struggled to comprehend wasn't mine.

I shook my head. "Never mind. What's the homework assignment? You have to boss me around in the bedroom?"

Sasha flinched and subtly increased the distance between us. Realizing my abrupt tone must have come across as harsh, I placed my hand on her thigh and gently squeezed. "Sorry. That came out wrong. Tell me what Annie said, please. I'd like to know."

My wife studied my face, assessing my sincerity. I waited patiently. As difficult as this situation had been for me, it hadn't been any easier for her.

"The first exercise involves touch but no penetration." Sasha paused for my reaction. I simply waited for her explanation, saying nothing.

"Annie said this exercise is to reduce sexual anxiety and refocus our senses on the pleasure of touch." Another expectant look from Sasha.

"How do we do that?" I obliged her by asking.

"We take turns touching each other with our hands and fingers for one hour. The point is not to arouse but to refamiliarize ourselves with each other's bodies," she said.

Intrigued now, I asked, "How does this help you be more assertive?"

Sasha drummed her fingers on her thigh. "The person receiving the touch has to give directions to the giver, I think."

"So the receiver is the one in control?" I asked.

Sasha's expression turned a weird combination of discomfort and confusion. "Not really. I don't know how to explain it. The receiver can give nonverbal clues about the touch and can even direct the toucher's hands to where they want to be touched, as long as it isn't the breasts or genitals."

"Nonverbal. So no talking?" I asked.

Sasha nodded, her lip curled and her forehead wrinkled. "No distractions. No music. No candles. No electronics. Just you and me naked in a quiet room. The focus is supposed to be on our sensory sensations and building intimacy."

I thought about it, trying to picture it in my mind. On the one hand, it took the pressure to perform off me. I didn't have to confess my little issue to my wife. "Is this a one-and-done, every night, or every other night? What's the frequency?"

"Two or three minimum, but we can do more if we like. Annie and I will discuss this at our next session. She'll decide if we're ready to move to the next exercise. She said the process to work our way to full penetrative sex can take up to six weeks." Sasha bit her lip and her expression said she was worried about my response.

I shrugged. "If it takes six weeks, it takes six weeks. I'm in this for the long haul. Whatever you say goes."

Sasha cupped my jaw. "Thank you. I wasn't happy when Annie said no sex, but she swears that the wait will be worth it. The method is called sensate focus, or something like that. Sex therapists swear by it."

I didn't care how successful it was. This gave me more time to get my shit together. "When do we start?"

"Tonight before bed?" She made it a question.

"Is this you being more assertive?" I teased, my tone dry.

She thumped me on the chest and sighed. "We start tonight before bed," Sasha said, her tone and manner more decisive.

'That's better," I praised.

My wife narrowed her eyes. "I changed my mind about wanting you to join me and Annie. I don't need two of you ganging up on me."

I shrugged one shoulder and smirked. "Was never gonna happen so it doesn't matter."

The rest of the evening passed with lingering looks that lasted seconds too long. There was a tension, a thrum of sexual excitement that harkened back to our younger days when sex was a forbidden dream. I felt more relaxed with Sasha than I had in weeks, and I knew it was because she no longer looked at me with silent questions and confusion in her eyes.

Dinner was delicious. Afterward, we settled onto the couch and watched the evening news. Sasha and I shared similar political views but every so often her viewpoint on an issue managed to surprise me.

As bedtime neared, I looked to Sasha for direction. Over the last hour, I'd found myself getting antsy, ready to get this show on the road. My wife appeared oblivious. She'd picked up her tablet and seemed engrossed in a book.

I stood and fighting to keep impatience out of my tone and expression said, "I'm going to lock up and head up. Are you coming?"

Sasha glanced up. "Yes. Just double checking to make sure I had the details of the exercise correct."

So that's what she'd been doing. The tension in my shoulders eased. "It will be fine. If we mess up tonight, we'll get it right the next time."

The smile she gave me was full of self-depreciation. "In other words, stop obsessing about it?"

I gently massaged her shoulders. "Honey, you can do this. I have faith in you. Have a little faith in yourself."

She sighed and rested her forehead on my sternum. "Tonight has shown me just how dependent I am on you to take the sexual lead. Honestly, I'm a bit ashamed of myself for not realizing it sooner."

I kissed the top of her head and rested my chin on it, grateful she couldn't see my frown. "There is nothing wrong with being sexually submissive. I didn't mind taking lead." Preferred it, actually, but I didn't tell Sasha that.

Sasha stirred and kissed the underside of my jaw before pulling away. "I know and I love you for it, but it's time for me to pull my weight in every area of our marriage. Let's go up, prepare for bed, and I'll explain the exercise. I think I understand it better now."

I dropped another kiss on her lips. "You lead. I follow."

We each had our nightly ritual. I liked to shower off the stress of the day. Sasha preferred wake-me-up morning showers that filled the bathroom with steam. When I came out of the bathroom, she sat wrapped in a towel on the side of our bed, playing with her phone.

"We can do two thirty-minute sessions or four fifteen-minute sessions. I think shorter sessions would be better until we get the hang of things," Sasha said.

"I agree."

"The exercise is simple. I told you some of the rules. No talking. No distractions. No touching of the breasts or genitals. This is the part I missed. When you're touching me, your focus is on pleasing yourself and my focus is to be on the sensations I feel."

I angled my head, a frown of confusion on my face. "I don't understand."

Sasha's face took on that intent expression she got when she tried explaining something she didn't fully understand. "Usually, when we make love, your focus is on arousing me, right?"

I nodded.

"That means you're more focused on me and my reactions than you are on your own pleasure."

"Of course," I agreed.

Sasha slowly nodded as a look of dawning understanding filled her eyes. "Tonight, the goal is simply for you to enjoy touching me, and my goal is to find pleasure in being touched. There's no thinking about or planning what comes next because touching each other in a way that brings us pleasure is the end goal."

Her explanation sounded simple but there was still a big question mark in my mind. "I think you should go first. I'm having trouble connecting the dots. Maybe it will click if you show me."

Sasha stood and dropped her towel to the floor. "Strip and lie face down on the bed."

I took off my sleep pants, climbed to the center of the mattress, and got into position.

Sasha crawled onto the mattress and knelt next to my prone body. Seconds later, I felt her fingertips on my back. She explored every muscle and groove. Sometimes she used the pads of her fingers. At others, she used the tips of her nails. It took a few minutes, but gradually I stopped trying to anticipate what she'd do next and started enjoying the feel of her touch. The sound of an alarm ringing was jarring.

"Time to switch," she announced.

I reluctantly sat up.

"How do you want me?" Sasha's voice sounded too loud in the quiet room.

I motioned for her to lie on her stomach. She immediately complied.

"I'm setting my phone alarm for fifteen minutes, starting now." Sasha set the device face down on the bed beside her. This was my cue to start.

Mentally reminding myself that the goal was not to arouse, I ran my fingers through her hair before pushing it to the side. Physically, I traced the outline of her body, starting with her neck and working my way to her feet. I noted the changes age and two pregnancies had wrought while I refamiliarized myself with her shape.

Women were so different from men. Soft where we're hard but containing a supple strength. My wife had curves and a few stretch marks where she'd gained and lost weight over the years. Her skin wasn't as tight as it used to be, but she was still sexy as hell. I loved every inch of her, especially her cute little feet. I was debating placing a kiss on the curve of her ass when the alarm sounded. Damn.

Sasha slowly sat up. Her eyes were heavy-lidded. With sleep or was it desire? "Your turn. Face up this time," she said, her voice husky.

I laid on my back. Sasha moved into position. She reached for me and stopped. "You're staring."

"Not watching you wasn't one of the rules," I reminded her.

"You're supposed to focus on the sensations my touch arouses," she reprimanded.

"I thought I was to focus on the pleasure. Watching you gives me immense pleasure," I teased, enjoying the way she flushed at my words.

"Grant, close your eyes and behave."

"Yes, ma'am." I closed my eyes and murmured, "If Annie could only hear you now, taking charge and issuing commands."

Sasha playfully slapped my stomach while giggling. "Stop. We're supposed to take this seriously."

I smiled with satisfaction but kept my eyes closed. I loved making Sasha laugh.

She placed her hands on my stomach, tentatively at first but gradually with more confidence. While her touch wasn't meant to be arousing, I felt my body respond. I let myself sink into the feelings. The knowledge I didn't have to do anything with my erection allowed me to relax and enjoy the heightened sexual awareness. It felt good. As much as I hated to admit it, Annie might be onto something with her harebrained methods. Time will tell.

All too soon, it was time to switch. Sasha's frontal view was more enticing than her back. Though the temptation was strong, I stuck to the rules, coming close to but never touching her breasts. Staying silent was difficult. I wanted to ask questions. Did she know how adorable those freckles on her chest were? How had I not noticed this sexy little mole on her upper left thigh? I wanted to kiss the lower belly pooch that she always complained about but was a reminder she'd given me two healthy babies. The more I explored, the more appreciation I gained for the marvel that was my wife.

When the final alarm sounded, signaling our session was over, I asked, "Can we do it again tomorrow night?"

Sasha crawled up the bed and joined me as I climbed under the covers. "Do you really want to, or are you just trying to please me?"

I cupped her chin with my hand. "I want to. I didn't understand the purpose of the exercise at first, but now I see its merits."

She searched my eyes to determine my sincerity before smiling. "I liked it, too. It wasn't easy to focus on what I was feeling instead of thinking about what I could do to reciprocate when it was my turn. I discovered I'm much better at giving pleasure than receiving it."

"We have all week to work on it," I assured her as I released her face and settled my arm around her waist.

"What was the hardest part for you?" she asked.

"Touching for touching's sake and not with the intent to arouse," I admitted.

"Huh. You're so physically affectionate, I thought that would be easy for you."

I grimaced. "It's different when you're naked in my arms. A different portion of my brain takes over."

Sasha laughed and snuggled close. "Tonight was good. I'm looking forward to tomorrow night."

I kissed the top of her head. "Me, too."

Chapter Seven

Grant

My phone pinged with a text notification.

Sasha: *Tonight's the night.*

Me: *Are you sure?*

Sasha: *Annie gave us the green light.*

Me: *That's Annie. What do you say?*

Sasha: *Yes!*

Me: *How do you feel?*

Sasha: *Excited. Nervous. Ready.*

That made two of us.

Me: *Tonight it is.*

I thought for a moment and then added: Don't cook. Let's go out. Put on something fancy. I want to show off my beautiful wife.

Sasha: *I'll be ready.* (Smile emoji)

Excitement and anticipation filled me along with a healthy dose of arousal as I set down my cell phone. Turning to my computer, I pulled up the website of the seafood restaurant Sasha liked. The place had a line out the door on weekends if you didn't have a reservation. I quickly reserved the last open spot for seven and got back to work.

A few minutes after five, I walked out of the office with a pep in my step, making my way to the parking garage in record time. Traffic was its normal stop-and-go, and it took ten minutes to reach the highway. Tapping my finger against the steering wheel, I finally made it to the highway where, fortunately, traffic was smooth sailing with no delays.

My thoughts turned to the weekend. It's been years since Sasha and I spent a lazy day in bed. Maybe I could entice her to linger with sex. We could lounge around, stay in our pajamas all day, watch movies, and make love whenever the mood struck. I'd have to call in delivery for lunch and dinner if I wanted to keep Sasha out of the kitchen. She was such a neat freak; cleaning one thing would quickly turn into a cleaning spree where she'd go through the whole house. Maybe I could even convince Sasha to carry our day of rest over into Sunday with a promise to help with any cleaning needed during the week. This way we'd both return to work on Monday, refreshed and rested.

Anticipation thrummed in my veins, and I had a smile on my face as I turned into the subdivision. It wouldn't be long now. That smile changed to a frown the minute I noted the car parked in the driveway. What was Wendi doing home? Thanksgiving wasn't for another two weeks. I left the car in the driveway since we were heading out. As I walked through the front entrance, I noted the piles of laundry.

My daughter and wife were in the kitchen. Sasha was bustling around, heating up leftovers from last night's dinner. Wendi sat at the table, fingers working on her phone while she chatted with her mom. Sasha saw me before Wendi did.

"Look who decided to surprise us," Sasha said, her smile beaming.

Wendi glanced up from her screen. "Hey, Dad."

I crossed to Sasha and gave her a lingering kiss full of the passion and intimacy we'd developed these last few weeks. When it finally finished–much too soon by my estimation–Sasha's cheeks were flushed and her eyes were glassy. Satisfied, I turned to this beloved child of mine whose presence had definitely put a kink in our plans. "What are you doing here?"

Sasha slapped me lightly on the chest with the potholder as she laughingly admonished, "Grant!"

"Gee, Dad. Nice to see you, too," Wendi said dryly.

I went to Wendi and kissed the top of her head in greeting. "Why are you here, and why didn't you call first?"

She wrapped her arms around my waist and gave me a tight hug, which I returned. "It's homecoming weekend," Wendi said as though the answer were obvious.

I crossed to the couch and set my briefcase on the floor. I'd take it into the office later. I shrugged off my suit jacket and loosened my tie, all the while studying my daughter. "I thought you made friends at school? Why are you hanging around with high schoolers?"

We'd allowed Wendi to take a gap year after graduation. The few juniors she'd been friends with had graduated last year. I had it on the best authority–Wendi–that no senior would dare be caught hanging out with lower classmen. There shouldn't be any former classmates she wanted to see, other than a favorite teacher or two.

Wendi laughed and rolled her eyes. "Yes, I've made friends, but a bunch of my high school friends were coming home this weekend, so we decided to meet up. I didn't call because it was a surprise."

I came back into the kitchen as Sasha set a plate of food in front of our daughter. Sasha stepped back and watched our daughter expectantly, ready to tend to her every need. I could tell my wife was in second heaven having our youngest home. Remembering the large pile of laundry in the foyer, I snagged Sasha by the waist and pulled her back to my chest. She immediately relaxed into my embrace.

I arched an eyebrow at Wendi. "Well, don't expect your mother to wait on you hand and foot. We have plans. Next time, call. Otherwise, you might walk in on your mother and me having sex on the kitchen counter."

Sasha made a strangled sound of disbelief and hissed, "Grant!"

Wendi choked on the drink she'd just put to her lips. After she finished coughing, she grimaced. "I'll keep that in mind. I don't want to be scarred for life."

To my scandalized wife, I said, "Our dinner reservations are for seven. Pack a bag. I'm booking us a hotel suite."

Sasha sputtered and turned to face me, her expression one of chagrin. "Oh, but I thought with Wendi home–"

"Nope," I said, interrupting her. We'd given our children nineteen years of undivided devotion. It was our time now. "Wendi, if you're still here, we'll see you on Sunday."

Wendi slid a sideways glance at the piles of laundry before turning a gamine smile on my wife. "But I was hoping–"

"That your mother would wash the two months of laundry you brought home? Not happening," I said firmly with a warning look at my wife when she began to protest. As much as I loved my children, I'd be the first to admit we'd spoiled them.

Wendi sighed and then eyed us speculatively. "You really aren't going to be here this weekend?"

"No, we're not, and don't think our not being home means you can have friends over. The same rules still apply," I warned.

Another eye roll. "I know, Dad. Geez, give me some credit."

"Good." I released my wife and stepped back. "Do you need money?"

Wendi perked up and held out a hand. "I never say no to cash."

"Of course not," I said dryly. I pulled out my wallet, removed two twenty-dollar bills, and dropped them in her hand.

Wendi wriggled her hand for more. "If mom's not cooking, I'll have to eat out."

"There's a refrigerator full of food, but nice try. Have fun with your friends," I commented as I closed my wallet and returned it to my back pocket. "I'm headed upstairs to pack."

I knew the minute I left the room, Sasha would give her more money. As I'd said, our kids were spoiled. I climbed the stairs, walked through the upstairs sitting area and into our bedroom suite. Now that our plans had changed, I decided to flow with it.

I called the downtown Hyatt that sat right on the river. Our company had a corporate business account with them and in return for sending business their way, they offered employees a discount. I booked my wife and I a suite for the weekend. The Hyatt had inhouse restaurants which offered room service. We wouldn't have to leave the room for anything. Perfect excuse to spend the day in bed.

Hmm, maybe I should thank Wendi for coming home unannounced instead of being annoyed.

Sasha entered the bedroom as I threw clothes into an overnight bag. I could tell by the tense set of her shoulders that she was annoyed.

"How much money did you give her?" I asked.

"Another forty. I can't believe you spoke to Wendi that way after she drove three hours to see us," Sasha fretted. She held her hands tightly together, a heartbeat away from wringing them.

Crossing to her, I took her hands into mine, and held firm when she would have pulled away. "First of all, our daughter did not come home to spend time with us. She came to see her friends. She wanted you to do her laundry. There's a difference." Sasha went to speak but I kept talking. "This is our time. We were great parents. We put the kids first and made sure they had everything they needed, even when that meant putting us on the back burner. They're grown now, and I want my wife back. Let Wendi do her own laundry. We have plans, and I'm not going to change them just because she showed up."

Sasha stared up at me, her gaze troubled. I could tell the moment she came to a decision. Her posture relaxed and a slight smile tilted one corner of her mouth. "You're right. Wendi came home, and I fell right into mommy mode. It's time we get back to who we were before the children came along."

I tilted my head and considered her words. "Maybe not the previous versions of ourselves. Young Grant was kind of a jerk. I prefer the more mature version of myself."

My words startled a laugh out of her. "You were never a jerk but given a choice, I'll take this version of you. He's sexy."

I drew back in mock affront. "Are you saying the younger version of me wasn't sexy?"

Sasha used one of her now free hands to tap her chin. "Young Grant was a hot commodity, and he knew it. That kind of detracted from his appeal. More mature Grant has a sexy confidence that stems from knowing who he is as a person and is not based on his looks. Confidence in a man is always sexy."

Despite our bantering tone, my heart swelled with the knowledge she still found me attractive. I slid my hands down her sides to rest on her hips. "Young Sasha had a lot going for her, but more mature Sasha is so sexy she turns heads everywhere we go. If anyone has aged like fine wine, it's you, babe."

She blushed and pulled away. "If we're leaving, I need to pack. Should I bring anything special?"

Just yourself, I wanted to say. Instead, I said, "The goal this weekend is to relax. Bring whatever you need to accomplish the goal."

"Yes, sir," Sasha said and saluted me before disappearing into the walk-in closet.

Her sassy tone had my cock twitching. Sasha and I had never played bedroom games. Maybe if I mention it to Sasha, she'd run it past Annie, and she could suggest a few as part Sasha's of homework.

*****

Almost thirty minutes later, I carted both overnight bags down the stairs, rushing a lagging Sasha out of the house. "We're going to be late for our reservations. You know how busy they get on Friday nights."

"You know I hate last-minute packing. I always forget something," she grumbled.

"It's not like we're leaving for a week. If you forgot something, it couldn't have been that important. You can do without it for the day and a half we'll be gone," I assured her.

I could feel her rolling her eyes as she said, "Spoken like a man."

I ignored Sasha's comment, focusing on the sound of the washing machine going. The pile of laundry looked smaller, telling me Wendi had taken me at my word. When I heard her leave earlier, I wondered if she'd ignored my warning. I was happy to see she'd done the responsible thing and taken care of her own clothing and not relied on her mother to see to it for her.

I escorted Sasha to the car, opened the door, and tossed our bags in the trunk after she was settled. We were finally on our way. To say I looked forward to spending time alone with my wife was an understatement. Wendi couldn't have picked a worse time to come home. I got under the wheel and reversed out of the driveway.

Once on the main street, I took Sasha's hand with my free one. "When you started this path with Annie, I wasn't sure how I felt about it. After spending the last four weeks doing the exercises, I'm glad you reached out."

"I wasn't sure what to expect but knew I needed to do something. You really don't mind the assignments?" she asked.

As I maneuvered through traffic, I answered her with an honesty I wouldn't have been capable of a month earlier. "I think they've helped more than our sex life. They've helped our marriage. With so many of our friends getting divorced, I was afraid it would happen to us, too. You seemed so discontent after Wendi left for school."

"Oh, Grant. I wish you had said something," Sasha said, turning to me. "I'll admit to feeling adrift, like my reason for being had suddenly ceased to exist, but I think all mothers feel that way when their chicks leave the nest. Being a mother took up a large portion of my time and energy for so many years, it took time for me to mentally adjust my priorities. Suddenly, there were all of these options available. Did I want to keep freelance accounting from home as a contractor or find a firm with benefits to work for full time? Or maybe a career change was in order? I even considered talking to you about fostering. I'd been a mother for so long, I wasn't sure I was ready to give it up."

At her words, I glanced at her in shock. I jerked my attention back to the road when a nearby horn blared. "Fostering?"

She laughed. "No need to sound so horrified. After researching the subject, I changed my mind. Fostering is a huge commitment. One I don't believe should be undertaken lightly and definitely not because I'm suffering from empty nest syndrome."

"Thank God for that," I muttered. "As for the rest, I'm on board for whatever you want. You want to work full time? Okay. Go back to school? We can afford it. Just say the word. Hell, if you want to quit your job and be a stay-at-home wife, I'm for that, too. As long as I'm a part of the equation, that's all that matters."

Sasha squeezed my hand. "You'll always be the most essential part. You know what I think I really want to do?"

"Tell me," I said, all ears as I navigated through traffic.

"I've been reading up on the state's Guardian Ad Litem program. While I definitely don't want to be a foster parent, I believe I'd like to be a voice for children in the system," she said.

As I listened to my wife detail all she'd learned about the program and its training, it was something I could definitely see her doing. Sasha was a compassionate woman, but I had reservations. "Are you sure that's something you want to do? I'll support you a hundred percent if you do, but I'm concerned about the emotional toil it will take."

"That's my only hesitation," she admitted. "There are some truly heartbreaking stories on Reddit. Still, I think I could help. Be a voice for those who need it most. That's got to be worth a little discomfort."

I mulled it over before speaking slowly, carefully considering each word because I could see how important this was. "I have no doubt that you would be great. These kids couldn't ask for a better advocate. If you pursue this route, I'll be with you one hundred percent. I'll be a listening ear and a shoulder to cry on. I only ask one thing..."

Her eyes held a glint of moisture, showing without words how much my support meant. "What's that?"

"Find a good therapist that deals with broken homes. Someone who understands the system to whom you can unburden yourself and that can provide wise counsel. I know my wife. You'd take the weight of the world onto your shoulders if you could. You can be their support system as long as you also have a support system of your own in place."

Sasha leaned over the seat and kissed my cheek. "Have I told you how much I love you lately?"

"You have, but I never tire of hearing the words," I said.

"Let's skip the restaurant. I want to be alone with my man," she said, resting her head on my arm.

"What about dinner?" I asked, in total agreement. Still, I couldn't let my woman starve.

"We can stop by the grocery store and pick up a few staples. I'm looking forward to a long, sweaty night. You're going to need sustenance to keep up your strength."

I felt my dick harden at the imagery her words evoked. "Your wish is my command."

Chapter Eight

Sasha

I stopped in front of our room, double-checked that I had the right one, and slid the key into the lock. The light turned green. I depressed the handle and opened the door. Walking into the room, I stepped to the side, allowing Grant entry. His hands were full of the groceries we'd purchased and both duffle bags. Seeing him hauling all of our things alone caused a brief surge of guilt but my offer to help carry them had been gently refused.

After Grant was inside, I closed the door and engaged the locks before turning to view our weekend retreat. Grant had booked us an executive suite overlooking the river. The suite had a dining room, living room, and a kitchenette with full-size appliances. The living room was a study in understated luxury, decorated in neutral tones of beige, tan, and gray with turquoise accents. The open curtains revealed a stunning sunset. When night fell, the lights of downtown and the bridges would sparkle, giving us an excellent view of the city's nightscape.

Grant set the groceries on the table before carrying our bags into the bedroom. I took the perishables out of the bags and placed them in the refrigerator. Grant met me in the dining room as I reviewed our dinner options. We'd picked up a few things from the deli. As he reached my side, I faced him and looped my arms around his neck. "How hungry are you?"

The grin he gave me held a mischievous edge. "That depends. What are my options?"

I toyed with his hairline behind his ear. "We could eat now..."

"Or?" he asked, a hungry glint in his eye.

"Or..." I said, drawing the word out, "we can wait until later."

Grant rested his hands on my waist, his expression thoughtful. "Which hunger do I want to satisfy?" he mused aloud. He arched an eyebrow and tilted his head. "Which way are you leaning?"

I pressed so close my breasts mashed against his chest. "What I'm hungry for has nothing to do with food and everything to do with you."

"Well, now... As always, I'll follow your lead," Grant said.

Smiling, I rose onto my toes and kissed him lightly on the lips. "In that case, do you have any final words before we get started?"

Grant dropped his hands to my hips and pulled my pelvis flush with his. "Just this. I love you. I have always loved you. I will always love you. You are my sun. My whole world revolves around you."

"Oh Grant," I sighed his name as tears pricked my eyes. "I love you, too. It's you for me. It has always been you and will always be you." I may have dated other men in college but my heart always belonged to him.

The kiss we shared was soft, sweet, and full of emotion.

When it ended, I took Grant by the hand and led him into the bedroom. A king-size bed dominated the space. Grant had set our luggage on the bench at the end of the bed. The beige curtains over the sliding glass door leading out onto a small balcony were open, but the sheers were drawn for privacy.

Turning to Grant, I reached for the buttons of his shirt. He caught my hands. "Timer, love," he gently chided the reminder.

Grinning sheepishly, I reached for the side pocket of my duffle and pulled out the digital timer. The lime green device looked out of place in our sedate surroundings. I punched in fifteen minutes and pushed the start button. The minute it beeped, a change came over me. Like Pavlov's dogs, I was wholly focused on what came next.

Under Annie's tutelage, we'd done this particular dance so often that the movements were as natural as breathing. No words were necessary. From this point on, we'd communicate everything that needed to be said with our bodies. There was a sultry sway to my hips as I walked towards him. The glint in his eyes stated he'd noticed.

This time, when I reached for the top button of his dress shirt, he did nothing to stop me. Grant stood still, hands hanging relaxed by his side. His intent gaze never left my face. I ignored him, my attention centered on the flesh slowly being revealed. The crisp fabric of his shirt felt cool and smooth under my fingers, contrasting with the heat radiating from his body. As Grant's sternum came into view, I placed my nose next to his skin and inhaled. He smelled like soap, spicy aftershave, and man. My favorite scent.

I took my time undressing him, stroking and exploring. There was no rush. We had all the time in the world. Annie's exercises had taught me that when it came to sexual intimacy, the journey was more important than the destination. Our goal was to savor every moment and prolong the anticipation. I wanted to kiss, nibble, and bite the flesh being revealed, but those actions weren't allowed on level one. So I immersed myself in the feel of firm muscles and hair-roughened skin. His body was a landscape of textures and each one invited my touch. The coarse hair on his chest and legs tickled my palms, and the smoothness of his skin made me want to linger with each stroke.

When the timer beeped, Grant's only remaining item of clothing was his boxer briefs. The outline of his shaft stood proud against the navy cotton, straining the fabric. I dropped my hands and stepped back. It was Grant's turn.

After resetting the timer, Grant lifted his hand and made a twirling motion with his forefinger. Spinning on one heel, I presented him with my back. He gave a murmur of approval. A tug loosened the halter tie of my dress, instantly baring me to the waist. One pull on the elastic waist had the dress pooling around my feet. The old me would have stepped out of it, scooped it off the floor, and set it to the side. The new me waited to see what Grant wanted.

A gentle nudge in the small of my back had me moving towards the mattress. The voiceless directions continued until I lay on my front with Grant kneeling beside me. I closed my eyes, awash in the sensation of his hands exploring me. The tiny beep of the timer was an unwelcome intrusion.

Sighing, I sat up and motioned for Grant to take my place. As I set the timer, I told Grant, "Level two."

"Level two," he agreed.

As I crawled on the bed to join him, I mentally chanted the rules. Hands and mouths allowed. No chest, breasts, or intimate bits. I lay on my side and drew closer until our bodies were flush. The next fifteen minutes were spent with me kissing Grant. Something I'd always loved doing. Soft kisses. Deep kisses. Licks and nibbles. His mouth was my playground, and I explored every centimeter of it. The taste of him was intoxicating, a mix of mint and something uniquely Grant. The time passed too quickly. The beeper sounded, and I withdrew. Grant followed me, attempting to continue the kiss. Laughing, I placed a finger over his lips. "Time."

With a muttered curse, Grant jackknifed up and lunged for the timer. He punched in the buttons and tossed the device to the side. I heard it clatter as he pounced, covering my body with his. Grant devoured my mouth in a hungry kiss. It seemed the leash was off. I lost myself in him. It was as though we shared the same skin. His weight pressed me into the mattress, surrounding and grounding me. Grant's hands roamed my back and hips, never staying still. His fingers traced patterns on my skin, leaving a trail of fire in their wake. I clutched his head, determined to keep his mouth on mine when it seemed like he would stray. The kiss gained a feverish urgency, yet his touch remained gentle. I could feel the restrained power in his touch. We both groaned when the timer sounded again.

Grant flopped onto his back, staring at the ceiling. His breathing was heavy.

I sat up, staring blankly into space. It took a bit to come back to myself. The timer. I needed to reset the timer. I glanced to the nightstand where the timer should have been. The dresser top was empty. I shifted to the edge of the mattress and gazed over it. The timer had landed on the carpeted floor between the wall and nightstand.

Retrieving it, I set it for another fifteen minutes and placed it near the lamp. I looked up to find Grant watching me, his gaze hungry and filled with anticipation. "Level three," I announced and peeled off my panties.

Grant's eyes darkened with desire as they roamed over my naked flesh. The heat in his gaze made me shiver. I crawled up his body and reached for the waistband of his briefs. Hooking my fingers under the elastic, I dragged them down his legs. Grant assisted by lifting his hips. Absently, I tossed the briefs to the side as I beheld the sight before me, and what a beautiful sight it was.

I ran my hands up the shins of his long, muscular legs, enjoying the feel of his scruffy leg hair. Men were so different from women, and I gloried in our differences. When I reached his knees, I indicated for him to spread his legs so that I could settle between them. Level three meant I could touch Grant's whole body. The objective was to explore, not to arouse. The only restriction was penetration.

I leaned forward and began pressing kisses on his thighs, working my way to his apex. He was so male. I loved his scent, his taste, and the feel of him beneath my hands. Using my lips and cheeks, I rubbed myself against him like a cat. Grant's hands shot out to grip the sheets when I gently cupped his balls and rolled them in my hands. The skin there was soft and delicate, a contrast to the firmness of his shaft.

I pressed my cheek against his erection, feeling its heat. I rubbed my face against the silken skin, fascinated at its bioengineering design. How could something so soft and flaccid become silk-covered steel and give so much pleasure? I ran my tongue over the veins and the ridge beneath the head. His skin tasted slightly salty, a mix of sweat and soap.

I rolled my eyes up to find Grant watching me. Hovering over the tip with my open mouth, I silently asked for permission. Grant's jaw clenched but he nodded. Immediately, I lowered my head, took him in, and simply held him in my mouth. The salty taste of precum met my tongue. I swallowed the saliva pooling in my mouth, and Grant snatched me off.

"Not going to last if you do that," he grumbled.

Knowing it was wrong of me, I laughed. I couldn't help but be pleased with myself for his reaction.

"Witch," he complained, but there was an amused glint in his eyes. "Give me a minute or this will be over before we start."

The timer beeped. The damned thing seemed to be moving faster and faster.

"Saved by the bell," Grant intoned as he reached for the device. When he set it down, his expression was predatory as he said, "My turn. Spread them, sweetheart."

Lying on my back, I drew my knees up and back, leaving my sex totally exposed to his view. The cool air in the room brushed over my damp flesh. Grant joined me on the bed and sat back on his heels, admiring me with a gaze that made me feel both powerful and vulnerable. Finally, he reached for me, his movements slow and deliberate. Grant's hands grazed my skin in a way that sent shivers down my spine. Every touch felt electric, each brush of his fingers ignited a fire within me. His touch was firm, yet tender, as if he were memorizing the shape of my sex.

My mind went fuzzy again with desire. The outside world didn't exist. There was only Grant. He took me on a slow sensuous dance as his hands roamed freely, exploring every inch of my body. My eyes closed as his lips latched onto my breast. He gently manipulated the nipple of one as he sucked on the other. The sensation sent bolts of pleasure through me, making me arch against him. Grant pushed one hard, muscled thigh between my legs, and I found myself arching against it. The friction felt good, so I kept doing it, not caring that it was against the rules or that my juices were saturating his thigh.

The timer beeped. Grant made to pull away.

"Don't stop," I ordered.

"The timer–"

"Screw the timer. Level four," I said, and pushed Grant onto his back. Our bodies became a tangle of limbs and heat as any thought of restraint was lost. We kissed with desperate fervor, hands stroking and clutching whatever we could reach. Weeks of self-denial had coalesced into this one moment.

I straddled his hips and reached between us with greedy hands. This had been a long time coming, and I refused to wait any longer. I positioned the head of his penis at my entrance and slowly sank down. We both groaned at the feel of it. My inner muscles clenched and loosened, only to clench again. When he was fully seated inside of me, I paused to savor the sensation. Then I began to move.

I rode Grant slowly, testing angles and adjusting the depth of penetration until I found an angle that made me catch my breath. Eyes closed, head back, I rode his cock. The pull and drag of his hardness against my sensitive inner muscles transported me to a world where nothing but my body and what was happening inside of it existed. Unconsciously, I picked up speed, rising and lowering faster and faster until I almost bounced in place.

Tension gathered, tightening in my core. I sobbed, straining to reach the pinnacle I could almost taste. Closer. Closer. Almost there. My body seized and on a choked scream, my body imploded. I was blind and deaf to everything but my core pulsing within. I don't know how long it lasted but when it finally faded, I slumped on top of Grant.

He flipped us over. Gripping me under my thighs, he raised my legs into the position he wanted them and sank inside. Then he drove into me like a mad man. I didn't have the energy to do anything but lay there and take it. With a hoarse cry, Grant stiffened above me, his body jerking and shaking as he came.

Still buried deep inside, Grant collapsed on top of me, giving me his full weight. He slowly released my thighs, and they dropped onto the mattress, the limbs feeling like dead weights. Grant ghosted his lips over the shell of my ear, murmured something unintelligible, and fell asleep.

Chapter Nine

Sasha

I don't know how long I dozed before I woke to find Grant staring at me. "What time is it? How long was I asleep?" I asked in a groggy voice.

We now lay side-by-side. His moving us must have woken me.

"Not long," he said. I didn't understand why he sounded so reticent. We'd just experienced one of the most amazing nights of our lives.

I reached out a hand and turned on the bedside lamp. Facing Grant again, I asked, "What's wrong?"

"Did you cum?"

I blinked in surprise. Couldn't he tell? On further consideration, I thought maybe he didn't want to assume. After all, for years he'd thought we were on the same page sexually only to discover that we weren't. I cupped his cheek. "Yes, but it wouldn't have mattered if I hadn't."

He frowned. "How can you say that, after all we've been through? You've spent months in therapy. We spent weeks doing exercises to make it happen."

My smile was gentle as I told him, "Yes, I did all of that to learn something I already knew."

Brows drawn together over narrowed, dark eyes, Grant grumbled, "And that is?"

I pushed my husband over onto his back and lay on top of him. "Intimacy is more important than passion." Crossing my arms on top of his chest, I viewed him somberly. "I plan to spend the rest of my life with you. One day we'll be old and gray, our bones thin and frail, and sex will be a fond memory. Because of my time with Annie and the skills she taught us, I have every confidence that we can be as physically intimate then as we are now, just in a different way."

Grant's expression softened as he listened. Wrapping his arms around me, he pulled me in close. "You're right," he said, his voice thick with emotion. "This was about us, connecting on every level."

I nodded, feeling a wave of love and gratitude wash over me. "Exactly. You're more than my lover. You're my rock, my anchor, and my best friend. I have every confidence that as long as we keep loving each other, we'll keep growing together, communicating and understanding each other. That's what really matters."

He kissed my forehead. I rested my head on his chest, and we lay there in a comfortable silence. After a while, Grant sighed. "In the interest of total transparency, I suppose I should confess a couple of things. You shared your secret with me. It's only fair that I share mine."

Not liking the sound of that, I tensed and sat up. "Oh?"

Grant gripped my hips. I had the impression it was to keep me from moving after he made his confession. "When Peggy left Tom, I wondered how long it would be before you did the same to me."

Head tilting to the side in utter bafflement, I asked, "Why would I do that? Peggy divorced Tom because he cheated on her." My eyes grew round. "Are you saying–?"

He surged up and gripped me by the shoulders. "No! I would never."

I searched his eyes before sagging in relief. I thumped him on the chest. "Don't scare me like that. What are you saying?"

Grant flipped us so we lay facing each other, our legs tangled together. "Tom's cheating was the final straw but both were discontent with their marriage long before that."

I froze, my thoughts going back to that time. Grant saw what I'd clearly missed. Peggy had been extremely critical of Tom. She'd always been a bit of a complainer, tending to see the negative where I tried to be positive. It was just her way, and when it came out that Tom had cheated, I figured she'd been justified.

"You two were closer than sisters. I heard the things she said about me. You never agreed with her assessment, but I wondered how long it would be before her words began to poison your mind," Grant continued.

Sighing, I propped my elbow up on his chest and rested my head on my hand as I looked down at him. "I wished you would have shared your concerns sooner. I could have put your mind at ease. Peggy and I had a huge fight about her attitude toward men in general and you in particular. I told her point blank that she could stop trying to turn me against you because it wouldn't work. The conversation you overheard was the first time we'd spoken in months. I haven't spoken to her since."

Grant squeezed my thigh in silent support, knowing how difficult a decision that must have been for me. "Because of me?"

I shrugged one shoulder. "Because of a lot of things. I don't like her lifestyle. I tried to be supportive, but the truth is, we simply no longer have anything in common. I like home and hearth and absolutely love being married. She's all about the party life."

"I want to be sorry because I know how much the relationship meant to you, but can't say that I am," Grant admitted.

"Thanks. It was hard at first until I realized I missed the idea of Peggy more than the reality of her." Changing the subject, I said, "That's one. What's the other? You said a couple of things."

Now a dull flush crept up Grant's face, and he fidgeted in a very un-Grant like manner. He took a deep breath, clearly gathering his courage. "Well, the second thing is... Those weeks that we didn't have sex before Annie pulled the plug with her exercises, I said I was giving you space. The truth is, we didn't have sex because I couldn't maintain an erection. My insecurities got the better of me."

I stared blankly, shock keeping me quiet. Grant had never had a problem in that area. As he'd gotten older, his frequency of hard ons had lessened, but he'd never not been able to get it up. "I don't know what to say."

"There's more..." he said.

I wasn't sure I wanted to hear it. I already felt guilty about what I'd put him through.

"I'm sorry I berated you for not telling me about your issue. Having experienced a sexual issue of my own, I can better understand your reasoning. I kept my silence because, one, I didn't want you blaming yourself for my issue, and two, I knew if I told you, you'd have pushed harder for me to join your sessions with Annie. The exercises she had us do weren't just for you. They helped me, too. Without them, I don't know how long it would have taken me to regain my confidence. Will you forgive me?" he asked.

"Of course. You don't even have to ask," I said.

His lips found mine again in a kiss. One kiss led to another, and soon we were making love again. Softer this time, a slow, sensual dance. Grant roamed his hands all over my body, shaping, exploring, and arousing. I responded in kind, my fingers tracing the lines of his muscles, committing every inch to memory. The world outside ceased to exist; there was only us, wrapped in our cocoon of intimacy and trust. Our marriage had survived a turbulent storm and come out on the other side, stronger and more resilient than ever.

Much later, we lay there, our bodies entwined, basking in the afterglow. I looked into Grant's eyes and saw a love so deep it moved me to tears. We had faced our fears and insecurities and had emerged not only stronger as a couple, but as better versions of ourselves.

"Thank you for being honest with me," I whispered.

He smiled, brushing a strand of hair from my face. "Thank you for being patient with me."

The beautiful moment was ruined when my stomach growled. Grant and I looked at each other and burst into laughter. He rolled out of bed, stood, and held out a hand. "Come on. Let's eat."

Later, seated at the dining room table with our foot-long submarine sandwiches and chips in front of us, Grant held up his can of soda. "Here's to us and a lifetime together."

"To us," I echoed, raising mine in a matching toast.

Epilogue

Grant

I collapsed on top of my wife, a sweaty heap of quivering flesh, gasping for breath. My heart hammered loudly in my chest, and my legs felt numb. I didn't think I'd ever come that hard in my life. Knowing I must be smothering her, I somehow found the strength to roll off Sasha and flop onto my back. The slight spring breeze billowing the curtains of the open bedroom window did little to cool my body.

Sasha lay beside me like the dead. Growing concerned at her lack of movement, I swiveled my head to get a better view. Sasha's eyes were closed and there was a smile on her lips. Her breath was just as gaspy as mine, but she was doing a better job of disguising it.

I slid my hand over until it brushed hers where it lay against her side. Reaching out a pinky, I snagged hers and asked in a raspy voice, "You all right?"

She gave a little hum before saying in a dreamy voice, "Never better."

That last round almost killed me but seeing that expression on her face made my potential heart attack worth it. My heart swelled with love and pride at her air of intense satisfaction.

Loud pounding sounded on the front door, followed closely by the ringing of the doorbell. I jackknifed up, adrenaline giving me a needed energy boost. "What the hell?"

The pounding started again. "Police. Open up!"

I surged out of bed. What the hell was the police doing pounding on my door?

When Sasha made to move, I barked, "Stay here!"

I pulled on my sleep pants and a robe and hurried downstairs, flipping the hallway switch as I passed. Despite my order, I could hear Sasha scurrying around. It took four steps to cross the foyer. Pausing briefly to punch in the code, I disabled the security alarm and snatched open the door.

Two uniformed officers stood on my porch. The female officer had her hand raised as though prepared to knock again. She appeared to be in her early twenties and from her spit-and-shine polish, I guessed her to be not too long from the police academy. The male officer was closer to my age. He stood a few paces back, obviously allowing her to take the lead but close enough to step in should his assistance be needed.

"Can I help you, Officer?"

Her suspicious glance took in my appearance. My robe was open, sleep pants slightly askew, and I was pretty sure my hair stuck up on my head from Sasha pulling it. In short, I looked a mess.

To her credit, the officer was all business. "We received reports of a domestic disturbance. Neighbors report hearing a woman screaming. Is there anyone else in the house?"

I thought of the open upstairs window and winced. The heat from a flush of embarrassment rode up my face. "My wife is upstairs."

"Can you ask her to come down, please? We'd like to speak to her. Ascertain for ourselves of your wife's safety. I'm sure you understand." The officer's tone said she didn't care if I understood or not. She wasn't leaving until she'd seen for herself that my wife was of sound mind and body.

"Sasha, you need to come down. The cops want to be sure I wasn't abusing you," I called out loud enough for her to hear me.

Sasha's "Oh, good Lord" echoed clearly in the foyer.

I saw the male officer smother a smile. The female officer still viewed me suspiciously. I hadn't invited the officers inside, and the position of my body blocked their view into my home. Clearly, in her eyes, this made me suspect.

Soon, the soft patter of Sasha's bare feet striking the wooden stairs announced her journey downstairs. Her hair was a wild tangle. With her flushed face, kiss-swollen lips, and heavy-lidded eyes, she was the definition of a woman who'd just had vigorous sex. She clutched the neckline of her hastily belted silk robe over her barely there nightie.

I adjusted my position to make room for her as she joined me in the doorway. Sasha hooked an arm around my waist, and I drew her into my side. "Can I help you, Officer?" she asked.

"Ma'am, one of your neighbors reported hearing screams. The report said it sounded like a woman in extreme distress." The female officer stared intently at my wife. "We're here to assist."

Sasha groaned and buried her face in my chest. Though just as embarrassed as my wife over the ridiculousness of the situation we found ourselves in, I still had to muffle a chuckle. "Officer, I assure you. I'm fine," my wife muttered, facing the officer again.

The female cast a glance in my direction before addressing my wife again. "Are you sure?"

Sasha clutched a fist full of my robe with the hand she had around my waist while never releasing the death grip she had on hers. "Positive," she gritted out.

The woman frowned. "We have people who can help–"

"Officer Daily, the resident has stated she's not in distress. Why don't you go to the car, write up the report, and let these good people get back to bed," the man said, stepping forward.

The argument I saw forming on the female officer's lips died when she met the senior officer's hard stare. "Yes, sir."

The three of us watched as the female officer stiffly stalked away. When she was out of earshot, the male officer turned toward us. "I'd like to apologize for my rookie. She means well but she's still green."

Sasha, ever graceful, smiled at the grisly old cop. "No offense taken. She was kind to be so concerned about my safety."

The police officer reached into his pocket, pulled out a card, and handed it to me. I released the door and took it. "Here's my card if you want to file a complaint."

I took it even as I said, "I'm sure that won't be necessary. She was just doing her job."

"Thank you. Enjoy the rest of your night." The officer took two steps away before turning back. "You know, I ran you on the way over. You've been married almost as long as I have. May I ask a personal question?"

From all of the crime television Sasha watched, I knew domestic disturbance calls were troublesome for police. They never knew what they were walking into. I wasn't surprised he'd investigated our address on approach.

Tilting my head to the side, I cautiously said, "Sure."

"You mind sharing how you put that look on your wife's face?" He glanced apologetically at Sasha. "Not trying to be intrusive, ma'am. I have a wife and I'd love to see that look of satisfaction on her face after we... Well, you get my meaning. Things get stale after a while. Routine, you know?"

I squeezed Sasha's waist and gazed down at her. She met my gaze and nodded. Smiling ruefully, I told the officer, "I'm afraid I can't take credit. Believe me. I wish I could. Last year, my wife consulted a sex therapist and what you see tonight is the result of a lot of hard work, deep conversations, and practice."

The officer rubbed the bridge of his nose with his forefinger. "A sex therapist, you say?"

"Yep. Sounds crazy but honestly, it was the best thing that ever happened to our marriage," I admitted, giving credit where credit was due.

"Huh, a sex therapist." The officer considered this information for a moment before asking my wife, "You don't happen to have her contact information, do you?"

"Sure. I can't recommend Annie highly enough. She's been a tremendous help to me. Let me get it for you." Sasha walked to the kitchen to write down Annie's contact information.

"A sex therapist?" the officer asked, eyebrow arched.

"Long story but trust me, it works. I was skeptical at first, but the exercises she prescribed saved my marriage. Now Sasha and I are closer than ever."

We fell silent as Sasha returned. "If you contact Annie, tell her I referred you. If your wife has any questions, I put my phone number on the paper. Tell her to call me at any time."

The officer held up the paper Sasha handed him and glanced at the writing before folding it and putting it in his pocket. "Thank you. Enjoy the rest of your night and next time, consider closing your bedroom window." He pointed up to where our windows were open over the garage.

"Thank you, Officer. We will. Believe me," I said with heartfelt assurance.

I closed the door. Sasha and I looked at each other and burst into laughter.

"Oh. My. God. I can't believe that just happened," Sasha gasped between fits of laughter.

I caught her by the waist and dropped a kiss on her lips. "Come on, wild woman. Let's go back to bed."

If you enjoy the Marriage in Crisis trope, keep reading for an excerpt of GAMED.

Author Note

I love seeing couples work through their issues to make their marriage last. I'd hoped my marriage would be like my tagline: Love that Lasts a Lifetime. Unfortunately, it was not to be. Now, I write to give my characters the Happily Ever After I didn't have. Also, to give myself and readers hope that true love does exist if we work for it.

A special note of thanks to my daughter, Erika Wynn Collins, for providing her expertise as a licensed marriage and family therapist.

For any reader experiencing sexual intimacy issues, I found the following books extremely helpful during my research to write this story:

Sex Without Stress by Jessa Zimmerman

Sensate Focus in Sex Therapy, The Illustrated Manual, by Linda Weiner and Constance Avery-Clark

About the Author

Zena Wynn is a multi-published author of erotic and sensual romance in various romance subgenres: Interracial, Contemporary, Paranormal, Sci-Fi/Fantasy, and Inspirational. She writes the type of stories she loves to read—stories with great characters who, through love and determination, overcome all the challenges that come their way. Her heroes and heroines are passionately, lovingly, devoted to each other. Zena wants her characters to stick with readers long after "The End."

To learn more about Zena Wynn, visit her website: www.zenawynn.com

Connect with her on Facebook: https://www.facebook.com/zenawynn.

Or contact her by email: zenawynn@yahoo.com.

Sign up for Zena's newsletter to stay up to date with future book releases @ www.zenawynn.com

J & M Consulting 2: Gamed excerpt

Jackie

Jake's office door was closed when I arrived at work the next morning. I cast it a wary glance before going into the breakroom. The next five minutes consisted of me holding my breath and my shoulders tensing every time I heard a noise. Finally, I exited the breakroom with a cup of coffee and Mike's favorite bagel.

His office door was closed, which meant he was inside. I knocked and kept one eye on Jake's door.

"Come in," Mike called.

I stepped inside and closed the door behind me.

"Morning, sunshine. I was just— What's wrong?" Mike's smile died. He stood and quickly crossed to stand in front of me.

I gave him a tentative smile, hoping he didn't notice the way my lower lip trembled. "Is that offer to talk still open?"

"Always. Sit down. You're shaking." He pulled me over to one of the seats in front of his desk. Mike and Jake had basically the same office set up, but Mike's was a slate gray with blue accents. They both preferred sleek, black modern furniture with mirrored surfaces.

"I brought you a bagel," I said, placing the bag on his desk.

"That's sweet. Tell me what's wrong?" Mike settled into the chair next to mine and faced me.

Holding the coffee cup with both hands, I stared helplessly at Mike. It wasn't my nature to go running to other people with my problems, but we needed help. Things had gotten beyond the point where I could continue to hope they would naturally work themselves out. With a sigh, I admitted. "It's Jake. I'm worried about him. He's not sleeping. He's drinking more than I'm comfortable with. He won't talk to me. I know something's bugging him, but he won't let me in."

Mike's face cleared. "Is that all? You know Jake and I were in the military. I told you a small portion of our work history. Most of it is classified, and frankly, it's ugly. Not something you want to share with the love of your life. Give him time. He'll work through whatever's bugging him."

I tightened my grip on the cup, needing its soothing warmth. "That's what I thought, too, until last night."

He tilted his head. "What happened last night?"

Leaning forward, I placed my cup on his desk. Then I unwound the decorative scarf I wore, revealing the bruises.

Mike jumped to his feet. "What the hell happened to your neck? You're saying Jake did this? Our Jake, the most protective man I know?"

Standing, I tucked a loose braid that had fallen free of my bun behind my ear. "Last night, we were playing around. I asked him about BDSM, you know, to help me prepare for our operation and... You remember that bag of sex toys Jake had on the island?"

"Yeah." Mike's eyes never left my neck.

"Jake explained what BDSM was all about, pulled out the bag of toys, and we decided to...play. It was an experiment to give me a taste of what I'd be walking into." I plucked at the material of the navy free-flowing pants outfit I had on while staring at the carpet.

"And...?" He growled the question, his voice deep and dangerous.

"It was fine. We were...you know, and then everything changed. At first, I thought it was part of the game until Jake flipped me over and ripped the mask off my face." I met Mike's gaze. "It was like someone flipped a switch. I don't know who was in bed with me, but it wasn't my husband."

I rubbed my arms, trying to warm myself. "Jake's eyes changed. Just before you guys got me off the island, I saw how Jake looks when he's in warrior mode. I thought his eyes had been cold then. I was wrong. This was arctic. There was no life in them. He wrapped his fingers around my throat and began interrogating me. I didn't know the answers, and I couldn't get through to him. It was like talking to a robot." I swallowed hard and touched one of the bruises. A single tear trailed down my cheek. "I thought he was going to kill me."

Mike cursed and raised a hand to run it through his hair. "Come here."

He hauled me close and wrapped me in a bear hug. I leaned into it and let myself cry. I'd been so afraid. Terrified, really, for myself and for Jake.

"What happened then?" Mike asked.

"I don't know. Something I said must have gotten through. He snapped out of it. When he realized what he'd done, he untied me, apologized, got dressed and left the house. I haven't seen him since." I rested my forehead on Mike's shoulder.

"Jake attacked you and then left you alone to deal with the aftermath?" he asked, sounding incredulous.

I sniffed and raised my head. "Yeah, that pretty much sums it up."

Mike cursed, long and vicious. Despite his obvious anger, his hand tenderly stroked my back.

"I'm pretty sure he's been having nightmares. Sometimes when he wakes, he doesn't know where he is. I've learned to be really still so I don't trigger him," I added.

Mike cupped my cheek. "Has he ever hurt you before this? Like when he's coming out of one of his nightmares?"

I shook my head. At his skeptical look, I elaborated. "He pinned me to the bed once, and if he'd had a weapon, I don't think we'd be here discussing it now."

"How long has this been going on?" Mike asked.

"Little over a month. Maybe two." I sighed. "Look, I understand that Jake has issues. His ex-wives warned me he wasn't an easy man to love. Hell, even Jake warned me. I've seen the reports. I understand about PTSD and flashbacks. What I can't get past is that he won't talk to me. Some days he's fully engaged, the most wonderful husband in the world. Other times, it's like looking at a blank wall. Physically, he's there but emotionally…? He disconnects."

Mike stroked under my eye with his thumbs, and I hoped it didn't dislodge the concealer and extra makeup I'd used to hide the dark circles. My makeup was water resistant to deal with sweat, not smudge proof.

"You know Jake loves you. Before I pushed the issue, the man was twisting himself in knots over you."

I took a step back and reached for my coffee. "I know Jake loves me, but if we can't openly communicate, what kind of marriage will we have? I'm not saying I'm ready to leave," I added when Mike opened his mouth to object. "I'm no quitter. I love him too much to give up on him the way the others did, but he's got to throw me a bone. Give me something to work with."

"The thing Jake loves about you is that you're not afraid to call him on his bullshit. Confront him. Don't let him get away with the silent man act," Mike said.

Books by Zena Wynn

True Mates Series
 *True Mates ++
 Mary and the Bear
 *Nikolai's Wolf
 *Tameka's Smile
 *Carol's Mate
 Claiming Shayla
 *Rome's Pride
 *Healing NeeCee
 *Alpha in Charge
The Nina Chronicles
 *Nina Chronicles 1: Nina's Dilemma
 *Nina Chronicles 2: Worth Fighting For?
 *Nina Chronicles 3: Loves Many Challenges
 Nina Chronicles 4: Full and Overflowing
Lycan Series
 *Seduced by a Lycan
 *Possessed by the Lycan
Fantasy Island Series
 *Fantasy Island: Mya's Werewolf
 *Fantasy Island: Cyn's Dragon
 *Fantasy Island: Fantasy Man
 *Fantasy Island: Moxie's Vampire
 *Fantasy Island: Zero Regrets
 *Fantasy Island: Star Fantasy (*Co-authored with Kioni Hall*)
 *Fantasy Island: Star Dreams (*Co-authored with Kioni Hall*)
J & M Consulting Series
 Played
 Gamed
 *Beyond the Breaking Point

Broken
Mate Match Agency
Mate Run: Pia
Mate Run: Cherise
Mate Run: Cara
The Question Saga
*The Question
After the Question
A Questionable Christmas
*Reyna's Vampyr
*To Jon, With Love
*Code-Switching ++
The Griffin's Woman
The Contract
*Illicit Attraction ++
*Trust Me Tonight
*Reclaiming Angelica
Uriah's Heart
Ryan's Obsession
Naughty Seductions: The Naughty Student
Naughty Seductions: The Naughty Husband
Marry Me (How Geeks Propose)

* Available in audiobook
    ++ Available in Spanish